STORIES
In the Key of
C. Minor.

Russell Bittner

CONTENTS

To Mary Anne Schwalbe, *sine qua non.*

Fright Night

Fright Night

"You've got a pretty face, kid," you tell your boy. "A million-dollar face. Don't fuck with it." It's an easy thing to say when that face isn't yours. When your own face ain't worth anything even *close* to a million — you know it, he knows it — and so he has to wonder on what authority?

Problem is, you've also told him — no, *instructed* him — to forget his face and defend the helpless, the weak, women and children certainly, but also weaker bucks — when they can't defend themselves. Sadly, that's an authority he doesn't question — because it sounds right.

There are nights when females, kidlets, weaker males of all species just wanna have fun. Halloween is such a night for humans. Halloween used to be a night when pretty much anyone could have fun. Problem is, Halloween isn't much fun anymore. Halloween now calls out the primitive — and primes for punishment.

First in line for punishment is "pretty."

Your boy's now out walking the sidewalk with his girl. They're at least a year past trick or treating, so just walkin'. They're big kids now, quite content to walk, to talk, to pass the little kids by. She comments from time to time "Oh, how cute!" He snickers, remembers just a year or two ago when he also came out in costume. But he's a tough guy now — and yet *not* so tough. He stops the next little kid he comes across; asks to look into his bag of trick or treat; notices how the bag shakes a bit as the kid holds it out; notices how the kid's cat whiskers also tremble as the kid looks up.

Your boy's a tough guy — yet not so tough. He crouches down to eye-level with the cat-kid, looks at him and snarls. The cat-kid tries to snarl back, but it comes out all wrong, comes out in a sniffle. And then the cat-kid looks down at his silly furry cat-feet and begins to bawl.

"Oh, *stop* it!" your boy's girl says. She's an old-time Brooklyn girl, after all. She's a tough girl—not from these parts, not from this *newer* Brooklyn. She's from a former time, a different 'hood, another world view. And so *really* a tough girl—and not just pretend-tough.

Now he has to choose, and your time to counsel is past. He's at least a year out of costume—too old to dress up, too old to have a parent-guardian, yet still not old enough to chuck the nest. Problem is—right now, this girl, this young boy in costume, these streets, this night, this moment—he has to choose.

He hesitates for a moment, but the cat-kid doesn't look up. The cat-kid fidgets with his trick or treat bag, then drops it to the sidewalk. He raises his cat-kid paws to his eyes, squats down and begins to bawl like a kid-kid.

Your big, tough Brooklyn kid hesitates no longer. He reaches down, scoops the kid-kid into his arms, raises him up into the air. The kid-kid stops crying. The kid-kid looks down at this big, tough bruiser kid who's now smiling. The kid-kid smiles back through sniffles. The big, tough Brooklyn kid grunts. The kid-kid squeak-grunts back.

Your big, tough bruiser of a Brooklyn kid puts the kid-kid back down on the sidewalk, gives him another snarl, then a meow. The kid-kid returns a small snarl, couples it with his own small meow, picks up his bag. The kid-kid wipes his nose, shakes his body one time, and growls.

The kid-kid, now once again a pretend cat-kid wanders off in search of more trick or treat.

Your big Brooklyn bruiser and his girl also wander off, and she pokes him once in the ribs. "Toughie," she says.

Your bruiser and his girl walk into Prospect Park; walk exactly one hundred steps up to the summit of Lookout Hill; catch a clear, cold, crystalline view of Manhattan's skylights tickling the ether; say nothing as he puts an arm around her waist, she puts one around his. They'll shortly be moving on to their own bit of trick or treat, and they can already taste the candy. Problem is, their Halloweens are well behind them—and they know it. There, off to the northwest, just across a river called the "East" and a bridge called "Brooklyn," are bigger, tougher, smarter, and richer kids who'll shortly test their stuff—and no doubt find it wanting. That's the *real* fright of this night—and the spirits of these two gently-tethered bruisers can no longer pretend otherwise.

The Poet &
the President

The Poet & the President

Of course I didn't hesitate when I got a call from his Executive Assistant. I'd never seen him before in person, though I'd seen his mug plenty of times on MSNBC and had even taken personal responsibility for getting it into corporate newsletters. He didn't, to my eye, look like a pleasant person. And so, I must confess, I took special pleasure in framing one particularly loutish headshot and inserting it at the top of his semi-annual "Letter from the President" to the lot of us underlings, his peons, but not—unless I could arrange to have it smuggled out—to shareholders or the press. I knew he never looked at internal newsletters, that he was far too removed to care about what happened day to day within the gates of his little castle by the sea.

And yet, I didn't hesitate when his Executive Assistant instructed me to take the public elevator to the ground floor, then to come back up via his private elevator to the penthouse. No, I honestly didn't.

I entered the antechamber—*her* space. She nodded without expression, picked up the phone to announce me—or at least, my arrival—waited an instant, then signed off with "Yes, sir." She then rose to open his door, looked me over with what I perceived to be a mixture of condescension and quiet rage—only a perception, mind you—and stepped back to let me enter.

"Thank you, Ms.—" I said with too much hesitation.

"—Etheridge," she inserted between this first forgetful *faux pas* and whatever might be my next fumble.

His office was half a floor large—and warm, toasty almost. At any rate, much warmer than what I was used to since he'd taken "green" measures to have the temperature turn down to 65° in the rest of the building. Three sides of it looked through tinted, floor-to-ceiling windows at the harbor, at Liberty, at the Verrazano Bridge off to the east, and—if he might occasionally care to glance in that direction—at Newark and Jersey City to the west. I shuffled up to within speaking distance, then waited for him to extend an invitation to take a seat in one of the two armchairs sitting at sedate angles to his desk, the upholstery of which suggested a long line of pretenders who might've settled in quite comfortably—even if just long enough to lose their heads.

No invitation was forthcoming. And so, I stood, looked, and marveled at the utter immensity of the man. This, I thought, is what they mean when they say "alpha male."

"I hear you're a poet, Biggs," he finally said—though without so much as a glance in my direction.

"Well, I don't know that I'd—."

"I've read some of your prosody."

I didn't know whether to feel flattered or terrified that he would describe my efforts as "prosody." The word had always sounded out of place to me—inflationary at best; archaic or antique at worst. Sort of like the armchairs. "Thank you, sir."

"I might be able to use someone like you. I, myself, write. Poetry, that is." The confession made me squeamish—like listening to someone confess to occasional masturbation. "Twice daily," he added, correcting my first impression that this might be a frivolous pastime. "The moment I step out of bed in the morning, and again before I turn in for the night." I was grateful he'd spared me any mention of composing while commuting, as I would've had to confess—out of solidarity, perhaps?—to my own habit of scrawling while on the subway. He chuckled. "Sometimes, even *en route* to the office if I feel I haven't polished off a piece to perfection. Even then, although the noise of the blades and of the tail rotor may wreak havoc with my meter, I compose."

"I understand entirely, sir."

This was a man for whom commas held no personal charm except to command by the force of their precision—once precisely aimed, that is, to deliver the greatest possible devastation to an adversary. And yet, I sensed that *my* part of this discussion was taking too long; that I was not pleasant in his sight; that I could easily be dispatched at any instant. My armpits grew damp in anticipation.

16

"Yes," he finally said with authority. "I could use someone like you. And so, I'm going to have you moved up to this floor. Installed right here next to me" — he nodded towards a door at one end of his office I'd not seen when I first came in—"so that I can summon you at will. How does that sound to you, Biggs?"

"It would be an honor, sir. Unimagined. Unimaginable, even."

"Well, start imagining. That's what we poets do, right?" he asked without waiting for an answer. "I'll have Lady Etheridge show you your new space," he snickered as if I, too, were on the inside of his inside snicker about his Personal Assistant. "Then arrange to have the contents of your present office brought up immediately. We'll get you some new business cards by COB today."

He leaned back in his chair, and I heard the shift of body-weight move over calfskin in a soft moan as he put the blunt end of a Montblanc to his lower lip. The nib looked to be of pure white gold; the barrel, of some material I couldn't identify beneath the lacquer. At the same time, I caught sight of a cufflink: a hammer on one side of his cuff; a sickle on the other. Both halves looked as if they'd been broken, machine-pressed, then soldered back together at a studied angle on miniature mounts that bespoke pure platinum. "We'll have to think of a title for you," he said as he gave a distinctly presidential tap to his upper lip with the Montblanc. "Whaddya think of 'Scrivener to the Chief'?"

I winced, yet managed to reel out a smile. I didn't know whether he was having me on or actually thought the wit fit. "Bartleby, sir. I'd be very flattered to be your Bartleby," I said, still holding tough to the smile — until, that is, it suddenly occurred to me that what I'd just said might've registered as flippant. He looked puzzled. "A joke, sir. Herman Mel—."

"Yes, I know who Herman Melville was. The man's buried at Green-wood, for Christ's sake. I fly over his mausoleum twice daily. He died poor, you know. Destitute—like his whales."

"Yes, sir. Like his whales."

"Still, you'd think they might've found room for him here at Trinity. He worked all his life right around the corner, you know—the IRS, or whatever it was called in those days."

"Yes, sir. At the Bureau of Internal Revenue—as I... I believe it was known in Melville's day."

That Melville had been buried at Woodlawn, in the Bronx, and not at Green-wood, in Brooklyn; that his simple gravestone was anything *but* a mausoleum—these were things I knew. I also knew he'd spent most of his adult life working at the U. S. Customs House here in lower Manhattan, and not at the Bureau of Internal Revenue.

Details, yes. But good men have been hanged for missing—or correcting for—such details. Or at least hung out, less a job and an income, to dry. I kept silent.

"By the way, Briggs, I intend that I shall not die like Melville. As a matter of fact, I'm no longer able to die like Melville. There are too many interests at stake."

"I see, sir."

He quickly pulled himself back into an upright sitting position and committed the nib of his Montblanc to the single sheet of paper that lay before him. It was—I could see at a glance—heavy bond, pearl in color, endowed with a watermark. He didn't bother to look up as he said, "Are you trying to suggest to me you'd rather *not*?"

"No, sir," I answered without hesitation—and yet desperately hoping he wouldn't notice the involuntary spasm that was lifting my heel up from the carpet into which it had only recently, and perhaps too complacently, sunk.

"Okay, something more prosaic then if you have any ideas. Let Lady Etheridge know what you come up with before lunch. She'll have your cards ready before you leave today."

"Yes, sir," I said. "Will that be all for now?"

"That will" was the last I heard from him that day and for some time to come. He'd been called away by urgent business overseas—this, according to Ms. Etheridge, from whom I was to hear only a "Good Morning" and a "Good Evening" in what remained of the workweek—as we perched and kept watch, like porcelain dogs in waiting, in outer offices to his main event. The "main event" elsewhere on the Street, just beyond our peripheral vision, was total collapse.

When I exited the "R" line that first Friday evening at the last stop in Bay Ridge, Brooklyn, I didn't hesitate to stop off at the local wine and liquor store to buy myself a couple of bottles before heading home. The Verrazano Bridge looked huge, blue-green and splendid from this vantage point—in contrast to the distant towers of lower Manhattan, grey-brown and almost toy-like in their remoteness.

I pushed open the front door of the End of the Whine. For just short of three years, I'd managed to pass by this Siren of a storefront with a smile and an old-timer's salute. But my new compensation, I knew, would allow me to reverse course—and, for the first time in my no-longer-upstart career, to peruse only the very best. I walked confidently up to the cashier and did just that—named a top-shelf bottle by its contents, then asked for a pair and paid cash.

Poetry—I was rather certain—was something I'd somehow manage to do without this weekend.

Collisions

"…[E]verything comes to us from others…. To Be is to belong to someone."
-- Excerpt from *Saint Genet: Actor and Martyr,* by Jean-Paul Sartre

Collisions

Maggie had read it once in a short story, "Androgynous," by I. B. Singer, and had committed to memory — "The real truth is this: The whole world is joy. Heaven is a festival all year long. Of all lies, the greatest falsehood is melancholy." But Maggie's memory and Maggie's understanding were two different things. She had a profound respect for Isaac Bashevis Singer and his stories, but neither her understanding nor her respect would allow her to overlook another simple truth — namely, that there's never only *one* truth for all people in all places and at all times. Maggie's truth? That she lived in a city and at a time of noise — and that her life was reduced to the barest essential: a competition for attention, which she was getting none of. One kind of attention, of course, could be had after dark and under covers. Her own fingers, however, were tired of paying that kind of attention. She wanted someone else's fingers, someone else's attention. When all is said and done — or, more precisely, when nothing is being said and nothing done — that's all any of us really wants or needs.

* * * * * * * * *

When she first saw him, it was, of all places, on the "R" line.

Morning after morning, once she'd descended from street level to platform, she'd turn immediately left and look back through a tunnel of sticky haze at stations behind hers for a pair of bright headlights, and would then either settle for text if there were no such headlights, or grow quietly excited if she'd timed her arrival just right. At this stage in her life, there was little else to compete with the excitement of a timely approach of headlights to her subway platform.

This morning, as on all others, she peered back down the track. Bright eyes met hers, and she felt the joy of timely arrival. No waiting, so sweating. Just on, off; transfer to express; travel forty minutes across Brooklyn and into Manhattan; get off again; ascend stairs back into daylight; walk a couple of blocks west; buy coffee and a donut; enter the elevator; arrive at her floor and exit; greet the receptionist; find her desk and settle in.

And then slowly, agonizingly, bone-numbingly, try to find a way to pass the next dismal eight hours without hating everything about her job, about her life, about the world, about her houseplants. This was the glory of living on the cusp of the MTV generation in the most exciting *über*-metropolis in the world in the most exciting century in history. And what, in the name of Ecclesiastes, could beat that?

The MTA could beat it—could beat it down to a sticky pulp.

But not today. Today, she had it licked.

The train arrived, but no one got off. There's nothing to get off *to*—she thought as she entered the car in front of her, found a space, opened her book and began to read.

Richard Yates's *Collected Stories*. Just a few weeks earlier, she'd read a rave review in the *Times*. The rave had made her feel, as raves often did, as if she'd been living in some kind of cocoon. How could she have ignored someone whom this editor considered to be "a writer's writer?" She prided herself on knowing who figured among writers' writers. And yet, the name of Richard Yates had not once run across her literary landscape. She held the book with reverence—but also with shame and a kind of amateur's pride. A dimple of her hoped someone would notice; the ironic grin of her knew no one would.

The story was good: *Doctor Jack-o'-Lantern*. One paragraph in, she was hooked. She suspected, in spite of the several bodies standing around her in congested space, that she'd be fully engaged from the point of entrance to the point of exit. A bit like sex, really. But this was only a *story*. And yet, so much more engaging than anything sexual she could recall—having very little to recall on this particular Monday.

The story was moving well. It had been written by someone she wanted to like—not because the reviewer had said so, but because this someone's world had said *not*. He and his work had been rejected, time and time again, but were now, finally, accepted. *Vindicated*. Yes! *That* was the word she wanted.

She was hooked by Yates's story, and she knew it. But she was also dimly aware of the approaching transfer point. This awareness would habitually find her making preparations to move close to the door so as to be first out, then first across to the express track and onto the "W" line.

She loved the "W" as no one should rightfully love a subway line. She loved it for its obscurity and for the sound of its name. Most of all, she loved it for its possibilities. The "W" was long-haul—like a Mack or Maersk, cross-country or trans-oceanic. The long-hauls had the time and patience to get into a rhythm—to settle down onto the tracks or into the waves and go the distance. With time, patience and distance, there was always the possibility of romance, and she lived daily in that hope. Each time she descended from street to track, with perhaps forty-five minutes to change her life from drone to polyphony, she lived in that hope. As the train moved from Thirty-sixth to Pacific, then from Pacific across the East River to Canal Street, there was time and rhythm enough in its sway to provide ample opportunity—or so she firmly and daily believed.

As the "R" pulled into the station, she looked out the window to find the "W" waiting. She smiled, closed her Yates, and crossed the platform to find a seat—or at least a *space* of potential romance.

During her short stay on the "R," she'd noticed someone out of the corner of her eye, had glanced over and given him a closer inspection. No. For her, he was much too pretty, much too tall-standing, entirely out of her league. And so, she'd gone back to her Yates—who, she figured, would instead make love to her with words.

She didn't find a seat. Instead, she found a reasonably comfortable standing position and settled in for the read, the rhythm and the ride. She decided once again, moving on, that he was good, this Yates–even if his world had dismissed him. She felt—the expression occurred to her as if in something like a literary dream—*the kindness of strangers*. Felt even that this was someone she could've had a single night with—and no feelings of remorse. His personal agony was right there on the page for any woman to see. A tiny bit of decoding, and he'd be in her gut. In his story-telling, she could read every chapter of his unhappy childhood, his thwarted adulthood, his screaming desire for recognition—or, at least, for attention—and then of his premature death. It was all right there on the page and swimming in alcohol.

She, herself, didn't drink. She didn't really understand drinkers' need for drink. She was almost ashamed to admit she loved the taste of water. Water—even when all around her the rave was for champagne, wine or bourbon. Occasionally, and as custom demanded, she'd take a nip. But she didn't really like it. Her need lay elsewhere.

She longed for love, but settled for water—and rhythm. As the "W" moved in fits and starts across the Manhattan Bridge towards the island that paid her rent, she settled back into the story of a child who would never provide her with love—but who, she hoped, might be able to tell her how to find it.

She read easily to the end of the page. Reading Yates's prose, she decided, was like skating on hard ice, her eyes a pair of perfectly honed and polished runners. Perhaps because the ice was too easy, too blue, she became aware of a competing tug for her attention, and let her peripheral vision scout out. Standing directly alongside her in the subway car was the man she'd seen on the "R."

Maggie suddenly became aware of possibilities.

Her heart began to beat faster. She felt a flush creep up from her breast to her neck like a slow mink on the prowl. She continued to see Yates's words and sentences clearly and to understand every one; but none of them stuck. And so she found herself re-reading the same sentences over and over again.

As the train moved onto the bridge, it would slow down, then lurch forward again. Each time this happened, she felt his arm brush up against hers. He seemed to be making no effort to quit the occasional contact—but neither was she. Finally, after an almost magical succession of jolts and lurches, his arm came to rest against hers.

She no longer even pretended to read.

With his skin against her skin, she could feel the warmth move like current from his body into hers. It was a power surge to her heart, to her head—and yes, to something down below.

He was leaning closer now, and she could feel the air from his nose—the steady respiration of it—on the back of her neck. He was also reading a book, and she wondered to herself whether the words on his page, to him, resembled the hieroglyphics on the page of her book, to her. Or was he rather concentrating so hard as to be oblivious of this accident of proximity? Would the arm that held his book leave *her* book-holding arm at the next turn of page? Worse, would he get off at Canal Street and leave her standing almost delirious with d—? Maggie dared not pronounce the word even in her own mind.

She tried to shut these thoughts out and simply concentrate on sensation. The first spark of recognition of his arm against hers had long since passed into something like a steady glow. At the same time, the rhythm of her breathing had grown shallow. She now became aware of a tingling sensation at the nape of her neck, in her nipples, in her ears—and yes, between her thighs. Then, of moisture accumulating—much like dew that after a long, cold night of abstinence might greet the sun of human contact. She shifted her standing position.

It seemed he hadn't turned a page in his book in some time. She wondered whether any of this was occurring in *his* mind, or if it was all still just an accident of proximity and a packed subway car.

She turned her head slightly away from him and noticed there were no other bodies even remotely close to hers. She then slowly turned her head back to where Yates would've wanted it and let her eyes once again do the scouting for her. There was no other body. The car wasn't packed—and hadn't been since the transfer point at Thirty-sixth Street. He'd *chosen* this position and was now standing firm on it—standing, in fact, directly next to her in a way that no one else had stood in months. He was there, clearly, because he wanted to be.

A whimper escaped her throat.

Can love start with a whimper? What long series of tremblings and shifts must first occur in the earth's core before the result is an earthquake or a volcano? How far would his arm have to move over hers to create the effect of shifting tectonic plates?

It didn't take long for her to find out. With the next lurch of the subway car, his arm broke stride with hers, passed over it and came to rest against her breast. Their books, too, were touching.

His arm wasn't moving away. Instead, it had planted itself in her garden. This time, it was no mere whimper, but a clearly audible intake of breath that startled her and the passengers in front of whom she was standing. At the same instant, Yates went tumbling from her hands. He stooped to retrieve it—a move that allowed them to look directly into each other's eyes.

He smiled as he handed back the book after first carefully dusting off the cover, then looking at the title and at the author's name.

"Thank you," she rasped.

"I believe Mr. Yates would be happier in these hands than on the floor," he said, slowly slipping his own book under his arm and taking both of her hands in his. "As I recall, Mr. Yates spent far too much time on the floor in his day—and likely never had anything so lovely as these to lift him out of his despair."

He was divine. Not only did he look like a god, he spoke like one. And he knew who Richard Yates was. No, not just knew of him, but *about* him.

Maggie's mind began to race forward. He could instruct her. His manner was clearly neither pedantic nor condescending. He spoke to her as he would speak to an adult, to an equal, to someone who'd understand him and his wit. The ecstasy now began to bubble up inside her and she felt . . . like a lava lamp. They would make babies together; they would build a house on the hill and fill that house with babies; she would garden and cook; he would help her — because he was clearly the helping kind; they would read together, and to each other; he would declaim and she would recite; and then, *she* would declaim and *he* would recite. Always naked — he would insist. And, of course, they would talk literature over breakfast, over lunch, over gardening, over dinner, and after sex. Until the children came along, they would eat all of their meals naked — *she* would insist. It was going to be . . .

Maggie suddenly realized he was looking at her as if it were *her* turn to speak. She blushed, put her hand to her mouth, and sputtered. "Oh, yes. Indeed. A drinker he was, wasn't he though." She couldn't help it. Whenever she found herself in an awkward situation, her Irish sprang up out of the ground and attached itself to her syntax like a marmot.

Now his look changed from expectancy to curiosity. She felt her freckles sinking into the blush like pebbles into quicksand and pinched her quivering lower lip with a thumb and forefinger. At the same instant, her eyes — like a pair of drowning sailors sighting one lone lifesaver — found his book. She reached out and grabbed it. "And what might you be reading?" she asked — and immediately wanted to slap herself with the one free hand now within easy reach of a blushing Irish cheek.

He took his book out from under his arm, turned it face up, and was about to tell her when the subway lurched forward. The action put both of them off balance. He dropped one hand from his book and reached up quickly to grab a strap. In the same instant, he noticed that she was tilting backward and about to fall. He dropped his book and reached out to grab her around the waist. As he did so, the subway jerked to a stop, and she slammed into him.

It might've been the most delightful head-on collision ever set upon by a subway car full of human eyes. This was no fender-bender. Had their bodies been made of metal, both would've been total wrecks. As it happened, their bodies were made of flesh — and his seemed to bend instantly into new shapes to accommodate the contours of hers. They discovered in the same instant that they were a perfect fit.

She'd never in her life felt so well-aligned. It was as if all of the preceding months of loneliness had prepared her for this harsh acquaintance, this brute collision. She didn't care that the other passengers were now staring at them. She didn't care that she was embracing a total stranger. She didn't care that they had exchanged no more than three sentences, and that every part of her anatomy was under full disclosure and on full alert. She just didn't care.

As the train started up again and eased down from the bridge into the tunnel towards Canal Street, the lights went out. All previous awkwardness or self-censure was swallowed up in the darkness of the tunnel. Maggie held onto him as if he were a thing of steel, as if he'd been made for this moment, stationed at this juncture between an empty past and an equally empty future.

Somehow he sensed it. Jorg—his name, though she hadn't yet asked it—was not a diffident man. Nor was he ignorant of the effect he produced on women. And yet, nothing in his demeanor, his attitude or his behavior projected haughtiness towards those who were drawn to him. He simply was who he was—and accepted his gift, neither in gratitude nor in indifference, for what it might allow him.

Their train pulled up and prepared to stop at Canal Street. He made subtle motions to get off. As only those who know the subway can understand, Maggie understood. She inhaled again—not an inhalation of passion, but of panic. She was still embracing an island. The island was about to sink. And until these last few moments on this particular "W," she'd known far too much of ocean.

She cut short his subtle motions and grabbed him harder. She didn't have an aphorism at hand, much less a plan. But *by God* she wasn't going to let him go.

He looked at her without flinching and took a moment to contemplate the offering. She wasn't really an unattractive woman, if also not precisely a beauty. Good color in her cheeks except where the freckles gave her a dappled look. Yes—that was it. She reminded him of a dappled mare: full and pleasant haunches; a robust breast; a thick mane. She'd be a good ride, he thought. And now was his time to put on the spurs.

"Where do you get off?" he asked.

She knew, of course, where she normally got off. But today wasn't normal. She decided she'd have to find out first where *he* normally got off, then claim that as her exit.

"It depends," she said, "on my mood and, of course, on the weather. I mean, whether I want to stroll a bit, window-shop," she lied. She hadn't strolled or window-shopped in years except for Maxi Pads and groceries.

29

With no one at hand to stroll with, why bother? "How 'bout you?" she asked.

He eyed her now with respect and no longer just idle curiosity. The bump in the dark was suddenly more to him than a mere bump. "My exit's Thirty-fourth Street, Penn Station," he lied, now eager to see how fast she could run unbridled.

She didn't pause. "What a coincidence! Also my stop," she said looking quickly away from a reflection in the window whose bare-faced lie she felt unable to abide.

Now *he* was on fire. "You know? I'm really not up to working today." He smirked as she looked up at him. "I feel a headache coming on."

She looked him directly in the eye. "Funny. I do, too."

At Fourteenth Street and, by some accident, now holding hands, they got out; descended a flight of stairs; walked under trestles; ascended another flight of stairs; then took their position on the express platform without a word. From the Queens-bound "W," they'd negotiated a U-turn on the same line and were now headed back towards Brooklyn and home — although towards *whose* home, precisely, remained unspoken.

They didn't have long to wait. This was why she so loved the "W." It came quickly, dependably, and often. And once she was aboard, it moved smoothly, rhythmically, lovingly. *Her* "W."

Maggie and Jorg took a seat, side by side, without the whisper of a space between them. Maggie was neither ample nor sparse, which is to say she was amply Irish, but sparsely Italian — her genetic cocktail. He was all Scandinavian sinew and muscle. They liked the feel of each other, and her charitable contours settled nicely into his tight spaces.

The car was practically empty. No one was watching them. He turned to her, looked into her eyes, lifted her chin as if she were a mere herring, and kissed her lips. Maggie's heritage, though sternly Catholic, wouldn't allow her to be treated like a herring. She grabbed his lower lip with her teeth and bit down. It was a mere yip. But he, a mere Norwegian, yelped. She laughed, but wouldn't release. Then she did a magical thing — as much for her, with this perfect stranger, as it was for him. She slid her tongue between his teeth.

It was as if the two of them had tumbled out of the train and onto the third rail. They were, in a word, electrifried — then adhered and slowly sizzled.

The train might now and again lurch or stop, or in some other unexpected way jostle them. It would, however, henceforth have no alternative but to jostle them as an item.

They rode this way, arm in arm and lip to lip all the way from Canal Street to Thirty-sixth Street. He breathed her air, and she his. The perspiration on their separate hands became one giddy sweat.

At Thirty-sixth Street, they separated lips but not hands long enough to cross over from the express track to the local, and from there to await the "R." They hadn't yet discussed destination. Maggie, with a natural instinct for nest-building, had already decided. She could — if he cared to offer her a present of food or other enticement — be persuaded to fly off to another destination. But she didn't need to be courted and wooed; she already belonged.

The "R" came, and they walked on — didn't bother to look for seats, as their exit was only a stop away. Instead, they stood and stared at each other for the length of track from Thirty-sixth Street to Forty-fifth Street, then walked out through the open doors of the subway car, up the stairs and out into sunlight to face traffic moving down Fourth Avenue in the direction of downtown Brooklyn and the bridges to Manhattan. They walked two blocks against oncoming traffic; turned left; then started up the hill towards Maggie's apartment.

Youth rendered the climb easy. The sun shone bright. The air lay brisk. The wind played in their hair like fast mallets on a xylophone. Their hearts, meanwhile, beat hard and deep like the bass groans of a pair of kettle drums. Throughout, however, they remained silent.

Jorg allowed himself to be led. Maggie, normally a flower upon most any wall, charged forward with her eyes and full attention focused on an imagined vanishing point in a tableau which, but for this man beside her, remained a wash of unfixed lines. She concentrated, kept all of the pent-up passion and anticipation of their love-making firmly inside, and would not let any of it be wasted on the spendthrift air.

When her building came finally into view, Maggie dropped Jorg's hand and reached into her purse. Like a mare now let loose to run, she quickened her pace. Her discovery of keys coincided almost perfectly with her arrival at the cast-iron gate in front of her building. She pushed it open and walked indifferently past flowers in glorious end-of-summer bloom, reached the front door, inserted the key, turned and opened. Only then did she look up and realize that Jorg was still a house and a half away.

She noted, however, that he could see her — noted, too, how he smiled in apparent tribute. She, in return tribute to her dogged, if not so athletic suitor, threw her purse down and reached up to the top button of her dress. She'd won the race, but she would gladly give up the prize. By the time Jorg reached Maggie's front gate, she'd loosened every button clear down to her waist.

When Jorg turned the corner inside the gate and came upon her at the front door, his smile evanesced. Maggie looked at him with mouth half open, cheeks flushed, eyes bright and dress flying at half mast. She grabbed his hand and pulled him through, then turned the latch to lock it. She led him by the hand directly through the living room, the kitchen, and into her bedroom. Only then did she stop to face him.

Jorg, dumbfounded, showed it. Maggie, always ready to accommodate, looked up at him and let a half-smile cross her lips. It was a half-smile of surrender, but also of camaraderie with this, her fellow truant. Behind it, and ready to burst forth like sun on a clear day's dawn, was the smile of every happy passion of which the human heart is capable, intended for him alone, if only he could now devise some god-like means to pull that sun up from its horizon.

"Maggie, merry Maggie," he whispered in her ear. "*My* Maggie."

He'd found it! The most glorious sound in the world to any pair of human ears, and he'd found it: her name. Moreover, he'd repeated it three times in succession and added possession to the repetition.

She threw her arms around his neck and put her mouth to his in equal parts lust and joy. She'd already known with something like absolute certainty she was going to make love to a man — and to a handsome man — that very morning. The knowledge had been sufficient to propel her on a homeward journey in which all else would be lost in white noise. What she could *not* have known — could only have imagined in her wildest, most untamed and unbridled fantasies — was that this man would take possession of her mind even before he took possession of her body — a body she was now only too willing to give.

When they broke off their first kiss a minute later, she opened her eyes, still only inches from his. Once again, no words were necessary, and yet a language poured out: a language that amounted to a poetry of reciprocal adoration.

Maggie stepped back. With the knowledge peculiar to her sex, she allowed herself to savor this last moment of anticipation. It was, she knew, the highest shelf of any love affair: a higher ecstasy than ten minutes before; a higher ecstasy then ten minutes hence. Ten hours from now, and certainly ten years from now, love would wear an entirely different habit. Its garments might be threadbare and worn, in some places quite comfortable and familiar and better than any new fashion. But this moment — in which this man looked upon this woman with the appetite of an army, in which she still remained, to him, a mystery almost as painful as it was exquisite — this was the moment, for her, of sweetest surrender.

As if slowly raising a white flag, Maggie lifted her dress over her head and let it fall to the ground, stepped out of her shoes, and paused. She wasn't wearing stockings or pantyhose — and so, had only two articles of clothing left to remove before her mystery would cease to be a mystique. Until this instant, Jorg had stood transfixed. He took her pause, however, as cue to prepare for engagement and immediately began to unbutton his own shirt, starting with the topmost buttons. She retaliated without hesitation, reached over and started with the buttons at the bottom. Their fingers met just below his sternum — her digits being far more dexterous. In no time, they had him out of his shirt, shoes, socks, pants and wristwatch.

They now stood before each other wearing only a facsimile of fig leaves. Her leaf still concealed the last vestiges of a mystery as well as an extremely precise barometer of her excitement. His was rather less successful at concealing much of anything. Maggie's proven peripheral vision could hardly ignore the clamor down below, and she smiled in gratitude at her personal good fortune — but also because it is a woman's natural wish to seek visible acknowledgment from the man she desires.

Jorg blushed.

Maggie's smile merely served to turn the heat up on that blush. To restore his demeanor to room temperature, she pushed up on her toes, craned her neck, and gave him a quick peck on the forehead. She then lowered her head just far enough to be at eye-level, and crinkled her nose. That did it: it, and he, were fully restored.

She put her fingers inside the elastic band of his shorts and began to push down. Only seconds earlier, those shorts had been a perfect tent — held in place with an Eagle Scout's attention to detail by the "trustworthy, loyal, friendly, courteous, kind, obedient, cheerful, thrifty, etc.," perpendicularity of Jorg's penis. Now, however, perpendicularity was about to concede to pandemonium. As for scout's honor — to hell with it in a perfect hand basket.

Then, suddenly, a snag. Maggie recognized that without direct intervention of some kind, the elastic band of Jorg's shorts would get hung up, and that she and Jorg might not get any further before winter. She didn't hesitate. She reached into his shorts, took hold, and lovingly pushed the cause of his snag up against his belly. His shorts now dropped easily to the floor, and Jorg stepped out of them.

The conspicuousness of Jorg's own excitement now made it seem as if there were three people in the room, one of them an impetuous child. This third party demanded attention and — rather than be put off by his demands — Maggie chose action. She reached around and unsnapped her bra. It slipped down off her arms and fell to the floor where both gravity and Jorg had long wanted it. She next reached into the elastic of her own panties and pushed them down over her thighs, knees and calves, at which point they dropped easily to the floor. She then raised herself again, slowly, to a vertical position and pulled Jorg onto the bed with her.

It might've been only a minute. It might've been an hour. To both Maggie and Jorg, time was suspended, and they took no more notice of its passing than they would the shifting of tectonic plates.

When they finished, however, one thing would've been clear to any of us: the sum created by the joining of these two was infinitely greater than their formerly isolated parts. Their simple joy in one another was the stuff of supernovas, the energy of Genesis, a left-over spark from the Big Bang. It was, in a word, divine.

As the laws of physics dictate, they continued the expansion of their universe all day long and well into the evening. It was only once their own, limited, *human* energies had been lovingly spent into exhaustion that Maggie suggested she would go and get something for dinner.

Jorg insisted he would go; the hunter-gatherer role was his. Maggie protested. This was, after all, her neighborhood; he needed rest. But she protested in vain. Jorg was up, clothed, and already halfway out of the bedroom when she, still naked, grabbed him from behind, spun him around, and put her lips to his with such force that he might've tumbled backwards to the floor had she not thought to grab the bedpost behind her with one hand and throw her other arm around his waist.

She did, and he was saved — and the coincidence was not lost on either of them. The second-most delightful collision ever witnessed by human eyes became, in that instant, their personal heirloom.

This, clearly, was a couple bent on collisions.

When they recovered from their near debacle a minute later, Maggie gave Jorg quick instructions on where to find Keyfood. This time, they cautiously made do with a quick kiss from lips to fingertips. Jorg then flew out through the front door, leaving it ajar. Maggie put on a robe, only then realized how dark it had become in her apartment, and turned on lights and the radio.

She would, this evening, prepare the dinner of a lifetime. Depending upon what her hunter-gatherer was able to bring back from the urban wilds, she would lavish on it, and on him, all the love, attention and art of which she was capable. She hoped he'd think to bring back a bottle of wine. Although long used to drinking water with her meals, tonight was a night for wine, Maggie thought—the fullest, deepest, reddest, richest a heart and palate could desire.

As she set about preparing the dinner table with her best and only silver, china and crystal, and with a pair of simple sterling silver candle-holders and her only two remaining candles, which she promptly lit, she allowed herself to reminisce upon the hours just past—almost as if the memory were already something more appropriate for a scrapbook, or even for a reliquary.

She couldn't believe her luck. Adrift for months in an ocean of no human contact, she'd found this island, this paradise, in—of all places—the subway. In *her* "W." Had it only been a dream? She sighed, thinking for a moment that maybe it had been just that. In the same instant, however, she suddenly felt something trickle down her leg. She giggled and ran to the bathroom. No, it had distinctly *not* been a dream, and she reached down between her legs with a wad of toilet paper to remove the lovely proof of it.

Jorg, in the meantime, was equally delirious in his own, quietly male way.

She was not exactly a beauty. Nor had he been adrift in the same sea of loneliness these many months. But there was something about this woman he couldn't quite put a finger on. She was not just another woman to him. She *embodied* womanhood. She was everything he could've desired in a partner. And he'd found her—of all places—on the subway. What irony, he thought, that he should find his woman—he was already thinking of her as *his* woman—on the "W."

As Jorg dwelt for a moment upon this singular thought, another interrupted it. This, their first dinner together, would not be complete without wine. He suspected she was not much of a drinker—also that she wouldn't appreciate or even know how to appreciate the difference between one bottle of wine and the next. But that didn't matter. He would seek out the fullest, deepest, reddest, richest wine the neighborhood could offer—price be damned!

He was now at the intersection and about to turn left around the block out of no whim other than convenience. Instead, he looked up and down the avenue for the bright neon of a wine and liquor store, saw one in the distance to the right, and jumped headlong off the sidewalk in its direction.

At that precise instant, Maggie heard a once favorite love song start up on the radio. She ran to it and turned up the volume—and instantly wished she could hold the song tight until Jorg's return. But this, after all, was radio. Instead, she danced to it alone—happy in the thought that she'd no longer have to dance to this or any music alone. From this night forward—she now thought, with her eyes closed and with just the hint of a smile on her lips, of her beloved O'Henry—*the pumpkins had* indeed *turned to a coach and six*. She leaned her head onto an imaginary shoulder; stepped up and placed her feet on imaginary feet; let the music move her and her imaginary partner around the living room. She was oblivious of everything else in the universe as she concentrated on the rhythm and the melody—and on the sway of her own body with that of her partner, her lover, her Jorg. Her thoughts braked briefly as they moved from O'Henry to Stephen Crane: she was no girl of the streets; but she might well be a girl of the subways.

The song came to an end, and Maggie returned to the kitchen to await her lover's return.

For a solid hour, she continued to allow herself the illusion she'd really found a lover, a partner, a soul-mate for life. The first time they'd made love, the sounds from her own throat had been, to her, like a thing out of the wild: unrehearsed, unexpected, unfamiliar and unmanageable. They'd come from somewhere deep inside her—from the heart of some beast for too long behind bars—followed by tears that seemed to know no end. The tears were her release of a loneliness that had kept her bound and caged for years. In letting them flow, without inhibition or shame, she was showing the front door to loneliness and isolation, bidding them exit from her home, from her heart, and wishing them farewell—but also never to return again.

Later, and after standing for an hour in the kitchen, when she imagined she heard a chuckle and a soft knocking at the front door, she knew it was neither Jorg's chuckle nor his knock. She already knew his laugh—full-throated and hearty—and suspected, too, that his knock would be neither soft nor sly, but proud, boisterous, unruly even. No, she knew *exactly* who'd just stepped around the corner and who was now at her front door expecting to be invited back in.

Maggie blew out the candles and took them out of their holders. She wrapped her silver back in its velvet pouch; put the pouch back in its own tiny hope chest; put the chest back in its place at the rear of her cupboard. She retired her only two crystal wine glasses back to their shelf, inverting them so as to keep the bowls dust-free over the coming months and years.

She then slipped out of her bathrobe, put on her nightgown, slid in under the covers and turned out her reading lamp. The room and her apartment were in total darkness except for the moonlight now having its own priggish way through her bedroom window. She put a wad of pillow into her mouth and bit down. Eventually, she fell asleep.

As the months wore on, days and nights began to resemble one another, and they all resembled the first. The only real variation in Maggie's routine was a steadily declining appetite—and with it, a steady decline in her attention even to water. Her gradual loss of muscle tone was something she hardly noticed, as she rarely used muscles for anything but the short walk from bed to table and back again. Nor did she remark that her voice had lost its timber as she had long ceased talking to anyone— including herself. But no matter. Even if by some miracle she'd managed to retain her voice, the lips with which she might've formed her words had long since lost their fullness.

Maggie had only one errand left, as she'd had only one real love in life—two maybe, but only one *constant* one. She resolved to pay a visit to her one constant love—and for this, she knew, she'd have to find the strength.

A banana was the only item of food left in her cupboard, and she ate it. It was well past ripe, but the softness of the flesh on her desiccated, blackened gums was a welcome relief. She took a glass down from the same cupboard and let the water run until it became free of sediment, filled the glass and forced herself to swallow most of its contents. She then lay down and waited for night. The skin around her eyes had contracted to such a degree that blinking came only with difficulty—never mind closing them for something as useless as sleep.

She didn't know exactly how many hours of darkness had passed— nor was there any visible migration of the moon to tell her what time it might be—as she got out of bed, felt around on the floor for clothing, and dressed herself. By the front door, she felt around again in the dark for an overcoat, gloves and winter boots. She was thankful that all of her clothes and footwear now felt two or three sizes too large, and that she could slip into them with a minimal expenditure of energy. She would need that energy, she knew, for the walk.

She opened her front door, then closed and locked it again. As she turned around to make her way to the front gate, she noticed that snow had begun to fall—and shivered as occasional flakes fell upon her face, melted and trickled down her chin and neck.

As she shuffled down the street, it occurred to her that she'd guessed right about the hour. Whatever activity there might otherwise have been at that time had now been chased indoors by the arrival of the snow. She'd meet no resistance and no curious onlookers.

A block and a half down to Fourth Avenue, then two blocks over to the Forty-fifth Street entrance, and she was there. She descended the stairway to a bank of MetroCard automats, paused in front of one of them, but then realized her vision had deteriorated to the point she could no longer make out the instructions. And so, she walked the few remaining feet to the attendant's cage, reached into her pocket, withdrew the last two dollars in her possession, and slipped them through the small opening. Eyes inside the cage registered the cash and gave back, without comment, a fare card. The transaction took place without either party's having registered the presence of the other—as neatly and cleanly as if two automats had conducted an indifferent electronic handshake.

She pushed through the turnstile, then walked slowly, deliberately down the steps to the subway platform and paused momentarily next to the tracks. There were no headlights to greet her—nor did she have any reading material. Instead, she used the predictable irregularity of the "R" to walk to the far end of the platform.

Upon her arrival at the other end a full five minutes later, she saw the first glimmer of headlights in the distance—probably three or maybe even four subway stops away—and took up the precise position at which she imagined the last door of the train would open.

Roughly fifteen seconds later, she felt the first chill winds blow against her face as the head car of the approaching train pushed the air through the subway tunnel ahead of it. Only seconds later did the train itself blast into the station. The sound to Maggie's ears, which had known virtual silence for months, was excruciating. But she didn't bother to cover them.

When the "R" finally came to a halt, Maggie discovered she'd misjudged her position. This was a night train—and so, a couple of cars shorter than she'd once been used to. The last pair of doors of the last car now stood open, but at some fifteen yards' distance. She knew she had only so much time to reach them before they'd close—making no allowance for misjudgments or slow-moving passengers foolish enough to be out at this hour.

She did her best to run towards the car, and had cut the distance by almost three-quarters when she heard the once-familiar double chime suggesting that the train's doors would close momentarily.

A sound of quiet desperation escaped her throat. She raced on and — as the doors began to close — reached out and stuck her arm through the rubber bumpers. The door jambs caught and held that arm in a lock-grip of wills: hers to enter; the conductor's to move on. She stood her ground and stared at the part of her body that was already inside the car, as if by staring hard and long enough, she could will the rest of her body to follow. After a few seconds' impasse, the conductor begrudgingly re-opened the doors long enough for Maggie to slip inside.

She immediately grabbed a handrail so as not to be thrown to the floor when the train, as it surely would, started back up with a jolt.

It did. She held fast and didn't fall.

As the train gained momentum towards the Thirty-sixth Street station, she walked the few steps across the car and positioned herself in front of the door, once again grabbing a handrail so as not to be thrown by a sudden brake.

At the Thirty-sixth Street station, she stepped out, walked across the platform and immediately looked to her left for the arrival of an express train. When she spotted two indistinct headlights, her heart began to race. As those same headlights grew brighter, she stared hard at the front window, still far in the distance. A single black letter against a bright yellow background was just beginning to come into focus - a collection of lines. Her heart raced even faster in anticipation until she realized that the black letter consisted of the wrong collection of lines: two vertical and a single diagonal. Before long, she could confirm that it was the "N" line — the *other* express train — and so, bound for a different destination.

She stepped back as the "N," like the "R" before it, entered the station. Apparently, none of the engineers in the MTA had yet been sufficiently aroused by the tormented decibels of steel meeting steel - whether of wheels against tracks or of brakes against wheels - to devise a more tolerable solution. New York was not, after all, Paris.

At this point, Maggie didn't really care. This was the "N" line, after all. She just didn't care.

She waited on the platform for the "N" to spit out and re-ingest a few passengers, then watched as it released its brakes and departed. The station was practically deserted. And now, for one of the few times in her life, she would have to wait for the arrival of her beloved "W."

She wouldn't have to wait long, however — of that, she was certain. Nothing else in her life had ever been so steadfast and regular as her "W." And now that the "N" had just pulled out, she could be almost certain the next express train would be her "W."

As she waited, two additional "R" trains came through the station. No one got off the first. A single passenger exited the second — but at the opposite end of the platform. There'd be no jostling for position once her "W" arrived, no competition for attention. The "W" would be all hers.

She looked again to her left and saw two headlights. They were still weakly shimmering — suggesting that the train was definitely in motion, and gaining speed by the second. Then she saw the single black letter against the yellow background and waited a few seconds longer to confirm its identity. Gradually, two distinct sets of diagonal lines came into focus: the double Vs of her "W."

There was no mistaking it now, and she smiled as she contemplated the train's timely arrival. Her heart raced only slightly as her arms rose up spontaneously in greeting. She stepped out of her boots and planted her feet on the edge of the platform. The train drew closer to the station, and Maggie felt the kiss of cold wind blow lovingly against her cheeks and through her hair. The rumble of the train's hard steel wheels against equally hard steel track grew louder, louder, louder *still* — clamoring for her as it had clamored for no one else.

The head car with its unmistakable pair of Vs was three seconds out of the station when Maggie leaned forward and left the platform. She now had the full attention of her one, constant lover — and they would not *ever* again be separated.

Enrique's Wine & Liquors, in bright red, was the last thing he ever saw. "*Cuidado!*" was the last thing he ever heard. Maggie's ruddy, freckled cheeks just after their lovemaking were the final frame in a rapid succession of mental images that flickered in his brain before it became just a mass of lifeless, gray matter. A car descending much too fast towards Fifth Avenue — "out of control" was how onlookers later described it to the police — slammed into him, lifting his body up into the air and hurling it across the intersection, through the plate-glass window of the storefront on the opposite side of the street and all the way to the back wall. There were few unbroken bones left in Jorg's body when it came to rest and slumped to the tile floor like a bloody rag-doll. It didn't matter. Jorg had been killed instantly, as the cerebral fluid inside his cranium was simply not up to the task of absorbing first the impact of his brain against his skull, then of his skull against the metal hood of the speeding car.

The car had continued on; had increased its speed; had disappeared into traffic; had never returned to the scene of what was now a crime. The drivers had never been found; the crime, never solved.

Maggie would never learn the details of Jorg's disappearance. He was unknown in the neighborhood—and so, no one could possibly have put the two of them together. She wouldn't have thought to go out looking for him until it was too late, until the ambulance had come and gone, until the police had concluded their report, until the crowds of gawkers had dispersed, until life on the street had returned to its selfsame, desultory pace. There was the matter of the storefront, boarded up overnight, and which Maggie would see only the next morning. But it was not within her power of conjecture to assume anything between it and Jorg's disappearance—at least not in the mental fog through which she'd already begun to drift by midnight of the night before.

By the end of the next day, even the plate-glass window had been replaced—as if no accident had ever happened, no crime been committed, as if Jorg had merely been a wisp of a memory. With no bones left behind, he was no longer even a relic.

Waltzing Matilda

Waltzing Matilda

Susan eased the charcoal-tinted window of her Ford Explorer SUV down slowly for effect. She wanted the officer to enjoy the full impact of her face, eyes, hair, neck and hint of cleavage through a lacy bra. She wanted him to take it all in *very* slowly, like catnip, one sprig at a time.

"No transit allowed without a minimum of two passengers," he said matter-of-factly, even if his eyes lingered unofficially on the lace.

"Officer, *please*. I'm already late. I've *got* to be on the other side in fifteen minutes."

"Sorry, lady. No exceptions," his voice snapped back to attention, taking with it his eyes. He then began to wave her quite officially out of the lane and back onto Tillary Street for access to the BQE. Her vehicle had just become another errant cow — and he, a horseless cowboy with a herd to move.

"But where—? How—?"

"Triboro Bridge. Closest access point for Manhattan-bound, single-passenger vehicles at this hour."

"The *Triboro*? But that's miles from where—! I'll never—."

"Move it, lady. Or park your goddamned van and wait until ten o'clock. Nobody goes over with less than two passengers before ten."

Susan had miscalculated—not once, but twice. She'd miscalculated in not taking the subway or a taxi. Now she'd miscalculated a second time in assuming she could negotiate her way across the bridge during HOV-only hours. Two miscalculations on a day she could ill afford to make any mistake at all. She absolutely *had* to be at Temple Street in twenty-five minutes, or her prospect would walk. No wiggle room. No margin of error for log-jams or traffic bottlenecks of any kind. Her prospect didn't know her, had never met her face to face, had not yet given her the chance to implicate herself and her cleavage in his mind. Her prospect had simply designated a meeting time and place by telephone. If she failed to appear at exactly nine o'clock, he'd walk. They always did.

She felt a single bead of perspiration drop from her armpit into the seam of her dress. Oh, God, now *that!* she thought. She squeezed her arm against her chest wall like an ink blotter, then glanced down at her dress to see if the single bead of perspiration had left a mark. Instinctively, she lowered her head and sniffed. Good. No stain, no odor. She glanced at her watch. Twenty-three minutes to nine. A bit of chaff formed at the corner of her mouth, and she snatched it away between two fingers. Jesus, she thought. Get a grip, girl.

The officer stood in front of her vehicle, hands on hips. She wasn't moving out of her lane fast enough to please him, and the line of cars forming behind hers was turning sullen. No one dared honk—not with a cop standing by. But the subtle revving of a car engine was an acceptable way to chide one recalcitrant cow without also running the risk of offending a cop. Several now began to turn up the RPM's in unison.

Just as Susan was about to swing out and away from the bridge, the image of a man entered her peripheral vision. He was apparently headed towards the pedestrian walkway in the direction of Manhattan. His pace was neither desultory nor hasty. Susan first noticed the predominance of leather—and that his shoes badly needed a shine. She didn't particularly like black leather on men, but it was a question of fashion, not an instinctive dislike. What she really needed was more time to observe and think. But the officer was waving her on, and the line of cars behind her was getting downright restless.

Susan lowered her window. "Excuse me?" she shouted over the roar of car engines behind her. The man didn't turn his head in any particular direction, yet he appeared to register her shout as a signal to him and him alone. Louder: "Over here." This time, he turned his head directly towards her vehicle. She leaned her own head out the window at a coy angle and let her hair cascade across the door handle. Then, without reflection: "Going my way?"

Susan immediately realized her error, but there it was, already out and said. Too late to retract or re-phrase it.

The man squinted at her, but otherwise remained expressionless.

"S'pose it depends which way you're going."

Susan didn't know whether this was an attempt at wit, or just stupid. She decided to ignore the quip. "Look, I've got to get across this bridge and into Manhattan in twenty minutes. They won't let me across unless there are two of us in the car. Can I interest you in a ride to the other side?"

This time, just the slightest smile formed on the man's lips. "To the other side? You mean, to the wild side?"

The line of cars behind Susan's was edging up on her rear bumper. The revving was becoming an angry chorus. The police officer rapped his knuckles against the hood of her vehicle and indicated the direction in which he wished her to move *now!* A bead of perspiration fell from Susan's other armpit. She glanced at her wristwatch. It was 8:40.

"C'mon, guy, I can't afford to quibble. If you're interested, jump in." In spite of her best efforts to remain calm and in command, he detected an edginess creeping into her voice. He liked that. He also noted the familiar "guy" — not exactly a word that fit well in this woman's mouth. A woman already of a certain age, he thought, and likely just a certain age for fun.

"Well, now. Maybe if you ask me *very* nicely."

At that moment, the officer abruptly pulled a memo book out of his hip pocket and marched up to Susan's window. "Okay, lady. 'Nough's enough. I gave you a chance. Now you can discuss it on your lunch hour with the judge."

Susan put on her most contrite face. "Officer, I'm sorry. This young man and I were just agreeing to share a ride over the bridge."

The cop looked the man up and down. "All right. Then let's get a move on." He put the memo book back in his hip pocket and perfunctorily pounded the hood of Susan's SUV as if to prompt it forward. Susan, exasperated, but with no more time or room to negotiate, turned her full attention to the man standing alongside her vehicle.

"Please. *Pretty* please. With a cherry on top."

The man smiled and skipped around to the rider's side of the SUV. He put his hand on the front door handle and attempted to open the door, but found it locked. Susan hastily looked for the universal power lock and threw it, but by that time he'd already moved to the back door, which he opened and entered.

"No, no, I didn't mean you should sit in the back. I just didn't realize—" Susan attempted.

"No problem," the man answered. I like it here just fine." He signaled to her with a flick of his wrist and forefinger. "Drive on."

Susan felt slightly nettled at the instruction. But with time running out, she settled for irony. "Certainly, sir."

They drove straight on in silence. She caught just the hint of cologne—Aramis, or something, she wasn't quite sure—and cracked her window. Traffic was heavy, bumper to bumper, and the going was slow. She glanced at her wristwatch: 8:45.

She felt a nervous tingle rise up in her from no place in particular, then noticed that both of her armpits had grown warm and damp. Still, she could detect no odor as she bent her head down to sniff first one and then the other. Her deodorant was clearly doing its job even on overdrive. Or maybe it was just the Aramis doing double duty.

When she looked up again, she glanced in the rearview mirror and saw the man smiling oddly at the back of her head. "Don't worry," he said. "You smell just fine back here."

Susan began to feel something vaguely unsettling, as if there were some other bad smell she could not identify or get rid of, and which insisted upon muddling her other five senses. At the same time, the man had started to hum and softly mouth the words over and over to a song she registered as something out of a far-distant past, absurdly out of season, and which began to grate upon her nerves:

> I'm dreaming of a w-h-i-t-e Christmas,
> just like the ones I used to know...

She settled upon talk as a means to clear the air and kill the tune. She looked again into the rearview mirror. "You live in Brooklyn, work in Manhattan?" she asked.

"Uh-huh."

"Walk to work and back every day over the bridge?"

"Walk on the wild side."

She ignored the comment. "Nice. Must be a good stress-reliever at the end of the day. Always the Manhattan Bridge, or sometimes the Brooklyn Bridge?"

"Yeah. Stress-reliever." he chuckled. "Ain't nothing relieves stress like a walk over the bridge." He didn't offer any further information about his preferred bridge of transit.

"It sure beats driving."

"Then why drive?" The man had a way of saying things that seemed to put Susan off balance. And yet, she wasn't sure whether it was really intention on his part, or merely social awkwardness.

"These windows are cool. I guess you can see out, but they can't see in, right?" he asked.

Speaking of windows, finally one of opportunity to get the conversation back on a lighter track, Susan thought, and she threw it wide open. "Yeah," she said. "Exactly that. Sometimes I make faces at people as I drive by, and they have no idea. It's a game I play by myself when I'm bored or lonely."

"Like one-way mirrors, right?" The kind they have in casinos on the ceiling and probably in lots of motel rooms. The guy at the front desk takes your money and gives you your room key. Then he smiles politely, wishes you a most pleasant and restful evening and goes around back to a false wall. On the other side of this wall, he's got a one-way mirror looking directly over your bed or into your shower stall."

The slightly unsettled feeling Susan had remarked moments earlier was gradually giving way to queasiness. "I don't know. I . . . I guess I never really thought about it." Looking for a way to detour the conversation, she had stumbled, giving the man just enough of an opening to squirm through.

"Never thought about it, huh? Tell me, do you play with yourself only when you're bored and lonely, or other times, too?"

The queasiness of seconds earlier now became outright vertigo. Susan fixed her gaze on the rear bumper of the car in front of her so as not to let her eyes catch sight of the drop to the water of the East River far below. Beads of perspiration under both arms were becoming rivulets. For the first time that morning, she could smell herself. She glanced at her watch, but failed to register the hour. She studied the speedometer and noted that the needle lurched only occasionally from zero to five as her foot skipped back and forth from gas to brake pedal. A furtive glance out her window at the Brooklyn Bridge, then at the Statue of Liberty beyond, informed her that she was not yet even halfway across the Manhattan Bridge.

She looked again at her watch: 8:48. She'd never get across and onto Canal Street in twelve minutes unless there were a sudden change in the flow of traffic. She was going to miss her appointment, miss her sale, maybe even lose her job. She'd have to give up the SUV, give up her apartment in the Heights, move out to Bensonhurst or Gravesend, for Christ's sake, or to some nameless corner of Queens. She'd be shunned by her friends, disowned by her family. Only her pet iguana would agree, lizard-like, to stay with her. And now she had this creep to deal with.

Why, *goddamn* it, hadn't she taken the subway or a taxi this morning?

she thought. *Why?* Because an SUV, like a Rolex or an American Express Platinum card — or maybe even just a Cross pen if you can't afford a Mont Blanc — makes a success statement to a prospect. This, the sum-total wit and wisdom of her Sales Manager.

She heard a clicking sound and realized that the man was playing with the child's lock on the door directly behind her, trying to pry it open with something hard and metallic that kept slipping out of the locking mechanism. She couldn't see the metallic object in the man's hand however much she angled her head to look through the rearview mirror. She reached down and rotated the automatic side mirror adjustment mechanism in an attempt to see the man and his metallic mystery thing, then realized she couldn't see back in through the tinted windows and promptly abandoned the effort.

In desperation: "The switch is up *here*. I'll pop the lock if you like. You think you might have more luck walking?" she asked brimming with optimism.

"Walk on the wild side, baby. Walk, walk. Wild, wild. Wild and weird, wonderful world, baby." The man's tone had become abruptly stentorian, the tight space of the SUV serving it like a canyon. "Don't touch a fucking thing. Just keep driving."

Once feeling unsettled, then queasy, finally vertiginous, Susan was now descending into delirium. Her SUV was moving forward in the center lane by inches at a time and directly behind a sanitation truck whose stench penetrated her vehicle's air circulation system and entered without possibility of exit. To either side, she felt squeezed in by a pair of dirty and rusting yellow school busses, a din emerging from within each that was matched in its ugliness only by the jeers of the schoolchildren as they pressed their faces up against the greasy fingerprinted windows and looked down upon the roof of her SUV. One of them actually put his mouth up to the quarter opening the window would allow and spit down onto her sunroof. Susan noted how the glob of spit stuck hard to the fiberglass. Behind her, and practically riding up on her rear bumper, was a cement truck. Although the morning light was bright, the truck's headlights were on high-beam, and they stared through the tinted glass of her rear window like two angry eels.

Without warning of any kind, the man reached up under her seat and released a lever so that the vertical half lost its brake, and she fell back into a semi-reclining position. With his other hand, he then took hold of a fistful of hair and pulled her head back hard against the head restraint. Her arms taut, it was with fingertips only that she was able to manage the steering wheel.

"Got children?" he asked.

"No."

"Married?"

"No."

"Got a boyfriend or a girlfriend, then?"

"Yes. Uh . . . uh, a boyfriend."

"Then I guess that means you get horny, right? But stay tight. Horny and tight, everything right—that's what little girls are made of."

The man plunged a blade into the leather top of the armrest between the two front seats. Susan realized what the metallic object was that he'd been using to tease the rear child's lock up and down: a stiletto with a retractable blade. The grip, seemingly of ivory, was the body of an absurdly buxom woman dressed in a kind of toga. Two transparent glass beads posed as nipples, quite pert. She stood upright, her legs slightly apart, sandals peeking out from under the hem of her toga, each one resting on the twin quillons of the stiletto's cross-guard. What Susan couldn't see was the trigger mechanism tucked somewhere up between the woman's legs. What she *could* see quite clearly was the figurine's ivory breasts and glass nipples, pointing directly up at her, the blade deep into the leather of the armrest.

In a panic, Susan reached out to unlock her door, but the mechanism wouldn't respond. She realized that the man had jammed or broken the power lock system with his knife. They were both now captive. Doors locked, windows up and locked. To all appearances, just a quiet gray beetle crawling forward in fits and starts somewhere on a bridge over a river, moving on over that river with the steel and glass canyons of lower Manhattan in the foreground and off to the left, a bright early winter sun reflecting hard back off the same steel and glass, but whose rays were muted as they passed through the tint of the windshield of this quiet, gray beetle inching its way to the island of Manhattan.

As if by instinct—some fight or flight kind of thing—she stretched her neck out and put her nose and mouth to the little bit of horizontal relief she'd facilitated moments earlier in an attempt to rid her SUV of the suffocating combination of Aramis, garbage, and her own disintegrating antiperspirant. It was a last, desperate gulp of breath before the vortex sucked her down. Eddies of fear and repulsion pressed in from both sides as the indefatigable, insatiable, unrelenting, deafening, blinding, blasting centripetal force claimed her, staked her, nailed her feet fast to the floorboards.

"Let's see just how tight, how firm we are, whaddya say, doll." As he pronounced the words "tight" and "firm," he squeezed her hair tighter and pulled her head back harder against the head restraint.

A gurgling sound escaped involuntarily from Susan's throat. "Please, Mister — ." He appeared to like that. Addressing a man easily ten years her junior with "mister." He appeared to like that a lot. The implied deference of it — and that she understood their respective positions.

"No, lady. 'Please' is how you asked me to get into your car, remember? With the cherry on top? We're already done with 'please.' Very soon, we'll be moving on to 'thank you,' thank you."

"What is it you want? I've got money. Not much. But I've also got an ATM card. We can find a machine just as soon as we get across the bridge."

"Do I look poor to you? Do I look like I want your money? Do I look like I *need* your fucking money? ATM cards are for bankers and other losers. I don't deal in plastic. No, what I want is chips."

Susan didn't understand where he was going with this. "Chips?" What did he mean by "chips?" Was this some kind of code, or slang, or street talk she'd never heard before on the fine cobbled streets of Brooklyn Heights, or was this his own private invention? "My *chips?*"

"Yeah. Like in a casino. With one-way mirrors. *Chips!*"

Susan held on to the steering wheel with one set of fingertips, unbuckled her shoulder strap seat belt and reached over to her purse with the other hand. She snapped her purse open and began to rummage around inside, though she really had no idea what she was looking for or even what she was supposed to look for. In the meantime, the man's grip on her hair remained relentless, and she was beginning to feel the strain in her neck muscles.

"Here, let me make this easier for you." He used the fingers of his free hand like a zipper to pop the buttons on the front of her dress from neckline to waste in one motion. The material fell back against her softly rounded, yet respectfully muscular shoulders, exposing her breasts inside of a lacy push-up bra. A silver St. Christopher's medal chuckled briefly at the end of a chain and came to rest on the bridge of that bra.

"Nice set o' *chips*," the man said nonchalantly.

Susan gasped. The world outside her SUV became a glutinous, whirling soup in her brain. She no longer perceived the vehicles in front, behind, or to either side of hers as solid objects. Even the bridge and skyline began to melt and dissolve into one viscid mass. She was only vaguely aware that the man's hand had left her dress and moved to the stiletto, which he withdrew in one smooth motion from the leather armrest. That vague awareness turned to ion-charged recognition, however, when she saw the dagger directly before her eyes, the blade pointing indecently down at her crotch. The man cupped the ivory grip with four fingers while his gloved thumb massaged the figurine's back. Susan grasped in the same instant that only action would divert this man from whatever sick little sideshow he had in mind for her — no, for both of them. Her eyes refocused past the figurine to the dashboard, then to the windshield and to the surrounding vehicles. She could hit the gas pedal and smash into the car in front of her, or she could hit the brake pedal without warning and hope the car behind hers would slam into her rear.

Either way, she hoped, she'd get the attention of someone outside. Blindly, irrationally, against all the evidence, against all the history of this city in which screams of violation and degradation tended, well, to get "lost in the shuffle."

The man suddenly rotated the stiletto up to a horizontal position and brought the tip of the blade directly to Susan's bottom lip. "Don't even *think* of parking here!" he hissed into her ear.

Susan wanted to crumple up in the seat and give herself over to childlike grief. But the man continued to hold the tip of the stiletto against her trembling lip.

"Time to accept Jesus as your personal savior, little darlin'. Ya know, on second thought — ." The man smiled. "Move into the right-hand lane."

Susan immediately dismissed the desire to crumple. Here was a command to act. She understood commands. She understood action. She put her blinker on and gradually edged her SUV over to the right-hand lane, as ordered. She could clearly see the East River below.

"Put the emergency lights on." She complied. "In thirty seconds, you're going to come to a complete stop and turn the engine off." The man began to count backwards from thirty. When he reached zero, Susan complied and turned off the engine. "Give me the key." She withdrew the key from the ignition and handed him her entire set.

The man re-inserted the stiletto into the gash in the leather armrest. Susan strained out of the corner of her eye to see him take the key ring between thumb and forefinger, then raise his still-gloved hand to his mouth. He grasped the lip of the glove with his teeth and pulled it back over the keys and off his hand, then took the leather ball of inside-out glove and keys and pushed it into the pocket of his jacket. His now ungloved hand reached out and withdrew the stiletto once again from the armrest. At a glance, Susan took in the long, spindly fingers—like raven's claws, nails bitten back almost to the quick. And cuticles red and white and raw—like fresh-cooked lobster meat.

"Now, let's take that stroll on the wild side."

Susan's only plan of escape had just been dashed, and her mind was blank. She was entirely at his command. They both knew it. And the bile born of helplessness and fear rose up from her stomach and settled on the back of her tongue. "Please, Mister—. Please don't hurt me."

"Don't you listen?" he shouted. "I told you already. We're way past 'please.' If I hear it one more time, I may just have to—*excise* it." With this, he jerked the tip of the blade across her lower lip.

"P-l-e-a-s-e-c-t-o-m-y," he hissed again in her ear.

The man removed his stiletto to a point six inches in front of Susan's nose and positioned it on an imaginary vertical axis. At the same time, he reached up under the figurine's robe with his pinky and pressed the trigger. The blade retracted with a snap. With his left hand, he continued his grip on Susan's hair, but gently pushed her head forward from the restraint. With the thumb and index finger of his right hand, he grasped the robed figurine by either side.

"Now, may I present Matilda?"

Susan stared at the figurine, but made no sound or motion.

"Be polite to Matilda, goddamn it, or she won't be polite to you!"

Susan blinked. "But what does she—do you—want me to do?"

"Be po*lite*, I said. That means, introductions all around. Be friendly. Offer her some libations."

Susan inhaled. "Hello, Matilda. My name is Susan. Can I offer you anything—to drink?"

Quite ironically sing-song: "That was good. Matilda is happy now."

"And I'm . . . I'm happy . . . to know that Matilda is happy."

"Do you know Matilda's favorite thing? I mean *second* favorite, really, after cutting and slashing and stabbing?

Susan tried in vain to suppress an involuntary whimper. At the same time, her eyes began to tear. "No, what is Matilda's second favorite thing?"

"Matilda likes to go waltzing," the man snorted. "Yeah, really. Waltzing!"

Susan attempted a smile through tears. "Waltzing Matilda."

"But first things first. And right now, Matilda is thirsty."

"Huh?"

"Be po*lite*, goddamn it! Offer her something to drink!"

"But I don't *have* anything to offer. Not here."

"You do, you do, you *do*! You have a milk-bar—and dispensers."
The man pointed with the figurine in the direction of Susan's breasts.

The suggestion hit home. "Oh, my God—."

"*Do* it. Matilda wants to drink, goddamn it!"

In quiet surrender, Susan unsnapped her bra. Her breasts fell gently forward as she squeezed her eyes shut. A couple of tears fell from the corners of her eyes onto her torn dress, darkly stained around the armpits. The man thirstily moved the figurine towards paydirt. As he did so, however, he drew the tips of his fingers as far back as possible so that he was holding the piece only by the folds of its ivory toga. Susan felt the hard contours of the figurine touch her skin. It was not cold, but rather warm—and clammy. As the figurine had been in the man's hand for some time already, this didn't strike her as odd. What *did* momentarily impress her was that she felt none of his skin against hers. He was touching her in a semi-private place, but through the medium of a robed, female figurine, under the ivory dress of which lodged a single stiletto blade. Neither the skin of his fingers nor the blade of the stiletto touched her. The only contact he sought was between her warm, soft human breasts and the warm, hard, somewhat clammy ivory breasts of the figurine.

The man nestled the figurine in under one of her nipples and began to make slurping sounds. This pantomime continued for perhaps a minute, during which Susan's mind began to turn as if on a potter's wheel, drifting through a dense fog between successive scenes. She first saw herself as a child, holding her favorite doll up to her own flat chest to let it suckle. Next, she saw herself in early puberty, bending down and pushing just the sprout of a breast up to her own mouth to taste the sensation of lips on a nipple. Next, she saw herself as a young teenager, her first boyfriend struggling clumsily to claim the prize of an early conquest. Next, her breasts now fully developed, on prom night her senior year in high school; the low cut of her gray, velvet dress holding them for display like two soft, milky-white mollusks peeking out over the mantle edge of their shells. The eyes of grown men—of male teachers, the dean, and even of the school principal—drawn to them very much against their responsible, *paternal*, adult will. (It was delicious, this power to attract older men; she suddenly had no use for her young date with his white carnations and Clearasil-covered acne.) Next, she heard her own giggle among a chorus of girls' giggles her freshman year in college, an evening with a bong, two or three or four classmates—she didn't really remember—all of them lying naked and silly and self-conscious in bed; nobody wanting to initiate, nobody wanting to terminate; the strange titillation of others' hard nipples against her own, also hard; against her will, against their collective will; yet no one able or willing to defy the natural, sensuous pull of warm bodies mingling. Finally, she saw herself as a fully developed woman with her fiancé, her breasts against his chest, both of their bodies heaving, both lusting, both searching for something beyond swells of fleshy pleasure and sufficiency.

The potter's wheel was slowing down. In her inner ear, her mind's ear, she thought she heard a click, a metallic swish and lock, and then the sound of gears grinding to a halt. With eyes still tightly shut, she perceived just the slightest twinge of pain in one of her nipples.

She opened her eyes. The man had released the stiletto blade and was teasing her nipple with it.

"Oh, plea—. Don't do that. Don't hurt me. I'll do— whatever you like. Just tell me why. Why *me*?"

"Matilda's happy now. Matilda wants to waltz."

"How . . . would . . . Matilda . . . like to waltz?"

"Barefoot."

"I don't understand."

And then he hit her with a blast of words. "No shit, you don't understand! None of you fucking-Yuppie-SUV-Roto Rooter-scumbags understand. This is pay-back, little darlin'. The rest of us out there? The ones you don't see, because your fucking SUV big-ass driver's seats are too far off the ground, your noses too far up in the air or up some other fucking-Yuppie-SUV-Roto Rooter-scumbag's ass to even take a glance. This is pay-back. Three cherries on the slot machine. I'm taking the whole bundle home with me. Then I'm gonna spread the wealth. Robin fucking Hood, they'll call me." Here, the man paused and took a breath to regain his composure and command. "But first, a little fun."

"Then it *is* about money. Perhaps we can come . . . to some arrangement."

"Oh, yeah. We can come all right, doll. But I don't know about any *arrangement*. You're not really in a position to *arrange* now, are you? *I'm* the composer here. I write the script. You just feed me the data. Oh, and by the by. Feel free to come whenever the spirit moves."

"What kind of 'data' are you looking for exactly?"

"Well now, I think we're getting the hang of this. A real feedback loop. Straight questions to straight orders. No detours by way of *please, please, please*, or *help me, help me, help me*. You learn fast for a Yuppie bitch. Data? Like, for instance, wha'd you lose on 9/11? Your cherry? No, I think we know that little pop-tart had already been plucked a long time ago. Money? Doubt it. Probably made some the very same day. Quick little investment in Bovis Lend Lease, a hedge hundred or two into Skanska, something like that."

"I don't invest. I don't make enough money to invest. I just sell real estate. Small parcels of land and buildings."

His sympathy for this brief, self-serving defense lasted the space of two blinks. "But more to the point: *Who'd* you lose on 9/11, huh? Friends? Family? Not likely. Oh, yeah. There *were* a few hundred of your kind inside, wasn't there now? A few hundred who got the big, crocodile tears on CNN, and whose mugs still look out from the front pages of the Times like little orphan Annie's. But fact is, most of the people who tried to get down and out the service entrance that day were nameless, fucking robots. Back-office people. Greencard-less, working paper-less, minimum wage GED'ers, if that. And let's not forget the few hundred coppers and fire jocks, stupid enough to be in the wrong place at the wrong time and not get the fuck out. All because some fucking white-collar maverick engineer had never considered—at least never thought to *inform* their sorry blue-collar asses—that when jet fuel ignites at 2,000 degrees Fahrenheit and the stacks of paper begin to burn-baby-burn, everything—and I mean *everything*—comes down. Sooner rather than later. And that you don't send a bunch of dumb Humpty-Dumpty blue-collar yellow jackets, each carrying over eighty pounds of gear, *up* the fire escape to a blind fucking death so that you can play out their heroes' hand over the coming weeks and months to keep people from asking the harder questions."

"I'm sorry, truly sorry, about those people."

"Yeah, I'll bet you are. I'll even bet you have your very own souvenir surgical mask, right? Hangs right there on the wall with some newspaper clippings from the day after. Whaddya you call that, a *montage* or something? I'll bet you got all weepy-eyed putting it together, hanging it up on your bedroom wall. Got some votive candles burning in front, right? Your big boyfriend comes over, you have a nice little glass of Chardonnay while he looks over your artwork. You get rid of your duds lickety-split, then have a little more Chardonnay while he looks over *that* artwork. And then you start getting all rabbit-like, him looking at you, the two of you looking at your *montage*. At the total fucking destruction. At melted steel girders and the spoiled meat products buried beneath."

"That's not me you're talking about. Not me or anyone I know." Susan for perhaps the first time in her life began to think outside of herself. "But . . . you? Did *you* lose anyone or anything? I mean, like, someone

57

close?"

"I lost a fucking dead-end job is all. I lost my way back over the bridge. But then I got entrepreneurial. And now I walk the bridge daily to remind myself. You know that word, I'll bet, 'entrepreneurial.' Or maybe you don't. You sell real estate, right?"

"I'm happy for you. But then, why — *this*?"

He sensed that she was getting a bit too cozy. "Okay, doll. This feedback loop is beginning to smell like Hallmark. You're really a nosy bitch, you know? *And* boring. All I know and all you need to understand *right* now is that Matilda is running out of patience. Listen carefully and see if you get this now: Matilda likes to dance in her bare feet. She likes to feel the floor under her bare feet."

"But your knif— your Matilda is wearing sandals. Ivory sandals. How can she dance in her bare feet?"

"Bare feet, bare floor. It makes no difference to Matilda. She just likes it bare. *Naked.* You with me *now*?"

Susan's grasp of the man's off-ramp way of thinking had gained exponentially in the twenty minutes they'd spent together in her vehicle. Soon, she realized, they'd require no words whatsoever to move from "command" to "obey." Her only wish was to remain alive and, if at all possible, unharmed.

Her vehicle was at a standstill. The emergency lights blinked on and off. Other vehicles behind hers moved quietly around to the lane directly to her left and passed by, not one of them stopping to offer assistance. Faces appeared through half-open windows; glared; searched briefly for information or entertainment; found none; stared dumbly or cursed at the reflecting glass for the bottleneck her SUV had become, and moved on.

Susan leaned forward, reached up first to one shoulder, then to the other, and pushed her dress down to her waist. Her bra fell to her lap. Several buttons sprang out, hit the dashboard, and bounced back to the floor. As she reached the juncture of waist and hip, just an inch below her navel, she hesitated and slowly turned her head in the man's direction as if to implore.

"Bare floor." He put a quick end to her pivot. "Those are the rules. Barefoot or bare floor."

Susan turned back towards the windshield and stared straight ahead into unfocused emptiness. She hooked her thumbs inside her dress and pantyhose as she kicked off one shoe, then pushed the other off with the toes of her now shoeless foot. Using her feet for leverage, she pushed her hips up and off the driver's seat and slid her dress and pantyhose down over her thighs, her knees, her ankles, and let them drop off. She continued to stare straight ahead, awaiting the man's next order.

Holding the stiletto in a vertical position, the man moved it from one breast to the other, then very slowly down towards Susan's crotch. He inserted the point just inside the elastic waistband of her panties, pulled them out to expose her pubic triangle, and held the elastic band in suspension.

"*Bare* floor."

The command was clear, even before he'd spoken the words. But Susan had wanted, needed, demanded, in her own turn, this one last *explicit* order from him.

As she had with her dress and pantyhose, she placed her thumbs inside her panties and pushed them down and off. They now lay on the floor of the SUV together with her shoes, dress and pantyhose.

The man abruptly retracted the blade of the stiletto, and Susan gasped. Was this a retreat? Was he finished? Had it merely been a bizarre game of strip poker in which he controlled the outcome of every hand by dint of his weapon and the subterfuge of jammed door and window locks? For one brief interlude in what seemed to her like time out of joint, she noticed the morning sun reflecting off some of the skyscrapers in lower Manhattan. Just beyond the tint of her windshield, the reflected sun shown brilliantly back towards the bridge, her SUV, and Red Hook. As it had *that* day, but for the filter of billions of dust particles blown into the air as buildings collapsed and went up, literally, in smoke.

With the blade retracted, the man again began to move his stiletto back and forth across her pelvis. After a series of horizontal swipes, he stopped and paused directly over her vulva. He dropped the piece slowly down until the stiletto's very hard, very male-contoured cross-guard made contact with Susan's very soft, lightly down-covered upper thighs. The figurine's sandals rested in the crook of Susan's legs, and its glass-bead nipples stared directly at the upper horizontal line of her pubis. Still, Susan noticed, the man allowed absolutely no contact between his skin and hers.

His next directive was unspoken, but firmly communicated through the movement of the figurine. He was fanning the piece gently from side to side, brushing up against one thigh and then the other. Susan tried to swallow, but all that remained in her mouth was parched fear. Perhaps his game had only just begun, she thought.

She parted her legs an inch or two. The man continued fanning the figurine a bit more persistently. Susan closed her eyes tightly and opened her legs until one knee touched the median armrest, the other, the driver's door. She felt hot and damp all over, but it was the hotness and dampness of terror. She could again smell herself as the odor of her body in distress filled the SUV.

A snap, followed by a metallic swish, and Susan knew the blade was out once again. The muscles of her inner thighs trembled violently as she felt an overwhelming desire to snap her legs shut and blunt the anticipated thrust of cold, hard instrument into her liquid soft, most tender parts. Just as suddenly, however, the nerves of those same inner thighs sensed a blow to the driver's seat, while her eardrums simultaneously registered how the blade first ripped, then penetrated, the seat-leather just in front of her vulva. The man's gloved knuckles inadvertently and almost imperceptibly grazed her pubic hair as he yanked his hand away.

"Now, drive on."

As precipitously as the delirium had overtaken Susan, it left her. She was in the driver's seat, naked, sitting in front of a fully clothed stranger. A stiletto stood upright between her legs. The scene was grotesque, absurd, yet somehow definable and manageable within its own peculiar context. She was still alive. She was not wounded. He had not physically violated her with any organ or any instrument. The only part of her body he'd even touched was her hair – and that, through a gloved hand.

The SUV was drivable. Manhattan was less than half a bridge away.

She conjured up an imperative voice: "Give me the keys. The car won't move without keys." The man reached into his pocket and withdrew the ball of inverted glove and keys. He held the whole lot out to her as he clumsily peeled back the leather with his own free hand to reveal her key ring. She took it, found the car key, inserted the key into the ignition, and turned the engine over. It started immediately. She turned off the emergency-light blinker and slipped the transmission into "Drive."

The SUV moved forward and joined the procession of morning commuter traffic into Manhattan. There was a more even flow now, and she thought she might be able to reach the end of the bridge and entrance onto Canal Street in a few, short minutes. What would happen to her and the man and her SUV once they reached Manhattan was anybody's guess. But that curiosity was at this moment entirely irrelevant. She simply drove forward, eventually easing again into the center lane so as not to have to see the water below.

From what seemed to be all directions at once, she heard the sound of police sirens. She checked her rearview mirror, but saw nothing. The man let go of her hair. She leaned forward and checked both of her side mirrors. Still nothing. She wondered whether the sirens were just wishful thinking and in *her* ears only.

"Keep driving," he commanded as he dropped to the floor behind the driver's seat.

Apparently not. They were real sirens. The man's reaction was clear evidence of that. Never had Susan found the scream of police sirens more comforting than in this instance. It was, to her mind — kneaded and beaten into a kind of infantilized pulp — like the sound of a posse on great white horses come to rescue her from the clutches of a vile villain, and she wanted to cry great, warm tears of appreciation.

Still, she could see nothing through any of her mirrors. Although the windows of her SUV were up tight and locked, the wailing of police sirens was becoming almost deafening. Sound, but no sight.

Just as Susan moved her foot to the brake to slow down and eventually stop her SUV, two police cars raced past to either side of her. The Doppler effect of their quick retreat worked as much on her spirits as it did on her eardrums. And what had just welled up in her eyes as warm tears of gratitude abruptly spilled over in cold tears of despair.

The man raised himself slowly from the floor, once again grabbed a clump of hair on the back of her head, leaned forward, and whispered into her ear: "Wild and wonderful! NYC's finest! Wizards on the warpath of death and destruction! I'm *really* sorry — aren't you? — they couldn't stop and pass the time of day. But you know? I'm in kind of a hurry myself. So *you* would've had to do the talking for both of us. And you don't really seem to be in the mood for talking just now. You really strike me as more of an action girl anyway."

As if she'd entered the wake of a speedboat, Susan noted even through the distorting cataracts of tears filling her eyes that the space in front of her was clear of all traffic. She accelerated sharply in a headstrong wish to sprint off the last couple of hundred yards of the bridge, maybe even to crash her SUV into the tower just short of the island of Manhattan only seconds away.

"Slow down, action girl."

She obeyed. The SUV passed under the bridge's tower and rolled onto the abutment on the hard granite of Manhattan. "*Mommie,*" she said to herself quietly for perhaps the first time in twenty years.

"Move to the curb right over there, action girl." The man indicated with his right hand, once again gloved, the spot at which he wanted her to stop. She obeyed, pulled up to the curb and stopped the SUV. She stared straight ahead, hands clenching the wheel, feet flat on the floor.

And then in sing-song: "I think it's time to say 'thank you,' for all your com-pan-y . . ." Susan nodded her head, but said nothing. "M-I-C . . . 'C'? Because we've *seen* your cookies. K-E-Y. . . 'Y?' Because we *love* the sight and sound and smell of you while you're baking. M-O-U-S-Eeeeeeeee."

The man reached down between her legs with his gloved hand, careful not to touch any part of her, grabbed hold of the stiletto, and paused. As they had once before, Susan's thighs began to quiver. She closed her eyes hard, and two new pools of tears emptied themselves from between her lids and streamed down her cheeks, over her breasts, and down to her thighs. Whatever had not been absorbed by her skin in its fast waterfall from cheek to groin disappeared into the grotto of her pubis. She did not see, but she could very much sense, the presence of the black gloved hand poised over the stiletto standing sentry between her legs. The muscles of her inner thighs screamed out to snap shut, but she couldn't obey their command. Not yet. Not while the ivory-robed sentry with her sharp, steel bayonet stood guard just an inch in front of Susan's exposed vulva, holding her legs splayed as if with invisible restraints.

The gloved hand, slowly and deliberately, withdrew the blade from the leather seat that had been its sheath. The gash, the wound in the leather, did not close as the blade came out. The gloved hand pinched the sides of it together like a pair of soft and swollen labia, and gently pressed each lip down. Once again the snap and swish, and Susan knew that he had retracted the blade. But to what end?

"Before she goes, Matilda would like to request a little souvenir to remember you by."

Susan kept her eyes shut, but forced herself to ask the question she knew he was waiting to hear. "What would Matilda like as a souvenir?"

"Matilda likes soft things. Not too wet and not too dry. Not too clean and not too dirty. Not too new and not too old. You're a smart action girl. Get smart and act."

Word games and riddles had never really been Susan's forte. But thirty minutes with this man had supercharged her mental batteries with his own very peculiar kind of current, and it was as if his thoughts and language had become hers by some sort of mystical, electrical transfusion. She reached down to the floor, picked up her panties, and offered them to his outstretched glove. He balled them up and put them in his pocket.

"Now, I believe, we've come to 'thank you,' don't you, Matilda? I believe that Susan would like to show her gratitude for this quite fun-filled interborough field trip we've shared today."

Susan's extraordinary effort to put a voice and sound behind her words resulted only in a hoarse whisper: "Thank you, Matilda."

"No, no, no!" the man said. "You've got to smile and open your eyes and *look* at Matilda when you speak to her! Don't you yet understand the meaning of the word 'courteous' after everything I've taught you today?"

Susan slowly and mechanically opened her eyes to see directly in front of her face the glass-bead nipples of the toga-clad figurine. Once again, and with excruciating difficulty, she opened her mouth and spoke. "Thank you, Matilda."

The man withdrew the figurine with a swipe and placed it in the inside pocket of his black leather jacket. "Well, I hate to eat and run, but duty calls." He put his gloved hand on the handle to open the rear door. The handle moved up and down, but the door wouldn't open. He pulled the stiletto back out of his pocket, snapped out the blade, then put the tip into the child's lock and pried out the stub of a wooden pencil.

It was to the back of Susan's head that he directed his last instruction. "You should *never* let children play in the car without first setting the child's lock and checking around for sharp objects. No, no, no!"

This time, he reached out to the door handle and opened the door easily. Sunlight flooded into the SUV in the three seconds it took him to exit the vehicle, slam the door, and vanish.

Susan sat motionless in the driver's seat. She heard the ticking of the SUV's clock and looked up at the console: 9: 20. Every muscle in her body felt as if it had been strained to the breaking point. She gave in to her exhaustion and collapsed onto the steering wheel. At the same moment, her urethral sphincter emptied her bladder onto the driver's seat.

In the same period of time, the man had walked quickly to the subway stop at East Broadway, had there descended to track level and taken the first "F" line to the other side of the East River.

Once in Brooklyn, he stepped out at the York Street station in Vinegar Hill, close to the Navy Yard. He saluted briskly in the direction of the Yard, then walked west the three short blocks to his apartment on Plymouth Street, climbed to the top floor of his four-story walk-up and pulled out his door key. On the door hung a hand-lettered cardboard sign — his little nod to Americana — which read: The Rock.

He opened the door and stepped in. He then closed and locked the door, turned on his PC and emptied his pockets. He opened the bottom drawer of his dresser and threw Susan's panties in with the dozens of others he'd collected on his excursions. (The man liked to think of his assortment of panties as a collection of athletic jerseys: the really good ones were pinned to a clothesline that spanned the hypotenuse of his one-room apartment from corner to corner; second-best got retired into the bottom drawer of his dresser; the not-so-good ones simply got dropped into a Dempsey Dumpster somewhere between the foot of the Manhattan Bridge and the subway entrance at East Broadway. Sometimes, the women had urinated in them even before he'd persuaded those same women to take them off. In that case, he didn't bother to take their panties home as souvenirs, and he knew the women wouldn't either. "Some of life's more special moments just can't be saved," was how he summed it up.)

One memento in particular, however — a single pair of very sheer cotton, pale emerald green in color with a couple of dark green pythons stitched into the seams and disappearing into the crotch — was an article he'd actually framed behind matte glass and hung at the head of his bed. As he prepared his little digital Eucharist, he genuflected soberly before the emerald green and made the sign of the cross with his own thumb on his own forehead.

He picked up the figurine and twisted the cross-guard. Out fell a tiny diskette. With lint-free paper and a can of Radio Shack's own anti-static spray, he carefully cleaned the glass bead nipples. With a flashlight, he then looked up inside the figurine past the blade and its release spring to inspect the connections between glass bead lenses and the tiny digital TV camera. All good and intact. He hooked the figurine up to a re-charger, then verified the connection and the flow of current. (When the connection was secure and the juice flowed, the glass bead nipples signaled the injection of current with a beep and a steady green glow.)

He next slipped the diskette into its tiny player. His PC had finished booting up and invited him to log on. He did so with his own password, "Pilgrim," and awaited a further command to log on to the 'Net. The pop-up appeared on his screen, and he completed the instruction set. Within seconds, he was on through his high-speed DSL connection, courtesy of a pal at Verizon off of whose truck enough spare fiber and backhoe loaders had fallen to get him hooked up to the trunk line that ran through Pratt Institute. In exchange, the pal got "sweetheart" access to his video library for life.

He then keyed in http://www.9/11Gold.com and scrolled down to the click buttons for "Members," "Guests," and "Producers." He clicked the third button and typed in his other password, "RobinGood," which gave him access to his account status, including number of visitors and subscribers current to the minute. The count was mounting impressively now that he was able to supply live-action material on almost a daily basis, and the hundreds digit of the pop-up counter registered loggers-on, even as he watched it, in rapid succession. Forget the tens and singles digits; they spun round in a whir.

This, he knew, was not yet a peak hour for viewership. Most Japanese eyeballs were too heavy either from excessive drink or from overwork to have an interest at this hour. India—for whose 1.036 billion this would otherwise be prime time—had limited access because of the dip-shits at VSNL who kept all the really good stuff to themselves. Ditto for the entire Middle East with its censor police—except, of course, for certain "privileged" clientele. In Europe, most folks were just finishing up a late lunch with a lover, or—lacking one—were on their way home to an early dinner with the wife and kiddies and wouldn't be logging on *en masse* for another few hours. When they finally did, however, varoom! (He could say a lot, statistically speaking, about late-night German viewing habits in particular.)

But on the East Coast—ah, yes—just after morning meetings, millions of instant needs for gratification and a quick, refreshing dip into his Coney Island cyber-thrill spill would translate into a huge spike just over an hour from now and just before lunch. By four in the afternoon, between East Coast on-the-job-boredom and West Coast lunch break, he'd practically be able to smell the ozone burning off the servers in Brno. "More eyeballs on my chickadies," he liked to muse, "than maggots on road-kill." Another spike would follow morning meetings on the West Coast, and then on into the night.

Our young man, in a manner of speaking, liked to think of himself as a modern-day astronaut. Not as the *old* kind, who would climb first into ill-fitting space suits, then into cramped capsules, then be shot up into God-knows-where for God-knows-what-reason to be mentioned in God-knows-what-perfuctory-NPR-salute-to-our-space-explorer-fucking-heroes—but as the newer, cutting-edge kind of astronaut. The entrepreneurial kind, who never had to leave his living room to circle the globe. And never in seven hours, nor in a sweaty space suit in a cramped capsule. Rather, in fractions of seconds, in satellite hops and fiber rings, in the comfort of his own "zone," providing fuel and entertainment—even *information* of a sort—to every one of the world's twenty-four time zones.

By four o'clock in the a.m., East Coast time, eyeballs had begun to dwindle. He was always slightly amused by the mini-spike indicating intense and disproportionate interest from down under, but Australia's and New Zealand's exceptionally zealous populations just didn't matter enough to his 'Net business for him to get all that excited.

He'd already had his ten-millionth visitor in less than two months. Life-time subscribers numbered in the hundreds. One-month and one-week subscribers, of course, were his bread and butter, and they numbered in the hundreds of thousands. He wondered whether this increase in traffic might be overtaxing the server, and made a mental note to have his pal, Bohumil, at Česká Televize, run another check on it at the cyber hotel in Brno. ***Churn is the Enemy of Progress and Profit*** was the title of a presentation he'd once attended at an industry trade show in Las Vegas, and he'd made the title of that presentation his mantra. "People don't like to wait for their cyber fix," the man reckoned. "The 'Net is not the fucking post office," he now and again snapped at Bohumil every time they came to loggerheads over the matter of further hard-Krona expenditures. It was the great cyber dilemma: whether to upgrade for growth, or simply cash out and move on to the next game in town.

Slow or not, customer retention was no longer the problem it had once been—now that he'd moved off the porn sites and onto 9/11Gold. com, where visitors and members alike could buy almost anything even vaguely related to that second day of great American infamy. He, personally, thought that some of the stuff was really in bad taste, and he occasionally felt a twinge of remorse about many of the vendors whose digital—if not exactly *physical*—company he was forced to keep by the nature of the business. (Some, he'd seen first-hand. But lots of it was very black-market stuff, and he didn't yet have the kind of disposable income that would buy him a key to those clearing-houses whose singular clientele consisted of very rich, very liquid, one-of-a-kind collectors.) And as the purveyors to those collectors liked to say: "to stare is human." God knows he'd seen more than his fair share of gawkers on and since 9/11.

Besides, in his mind at least, he was than just a vendor or purveyor. He'd invented a whole new genre of Internet *cinéma vérité* he liked to call "scratch 'n sniff" films. Nothing, he thought, beats fear. He knew it was only a matter of time before the forward march of technology would allow him to install a tiny microphone in his Matilda in order to capture audio— i.e., sighs, murmurs, groans, weeping, pleading, begging for mommies elsewhere in the night. Still, audio wouldn't hold a candle to the *ultimate* sideshow: digital smell. In fact, he already had a pal at IFF, Inc. working on it for him—in exchange for "sweetheart" access, doncha know.

And then there was the money. It was all flowing into a bank account in the Cayman Islands, untouched by human hands (including, for the time being, his own) until the day he was ready to give up his passport and buy an island in the South Pacific. His own entire freaking island. He'd never again have to worry about wearing leather gloves — not in the South Pacific, that was for sure. He'd visited an educational Web site or two in his time, and he knew that the temperature never dropped below 70° in the South Pacific. "Sure beats sweater weather," he often chuckled to himself, and also shared with anyone who cared to inquire about his exit strategy.

He clicked around the content providers' section of 9/11Gold until everything was in place for him to encrypt and upload the video. Then he keyed in a title for the trailer, laying the dark brown letters with black borders down against his favorite shade of pale emerald green wallpaper:

"Susan's Chocolate Chippers."

"Showtime!" he breathed to himself in imitation of Susan's hoarse whisper as he clicked on "Upload." As the pop-up giving him the bit-rate at which he was transmitting appeared on his screen, he began to sing an old Woody Guthrie tune:

"Believe it or not, you won't find it so hot
If you ain't got the Do Re Mi."

He figured he could cut, edit, label and archive on the fly. Reduce the lot to five minutes, then re-purpose the remainder for a rainy day. Maybe add some digital effects, new background, new players from other episodes. Nothing like re-purposing to goose the revenue stream, he sometimes mused to himself.

"Little darlin' Susie," he murmured to the still vivid memory of her. "I'm gonna make you a world-class starlet in less time than it'll take you to come back home here to us in Brooklyn and find yourself a fresh pair of panties!"

"Gray is nice," he murmured as he glanced reverently at the matte-glassed frame hanging over his bed. "But there ain't nothing, *nothing*, like emerald green."

In the Animal Kingdom

A Thanksgiving Story

"Mammalian life is social and relational. What defines the mammalian class, physiologically, is ... the possession of a portion of the brain known as the limbic system, which allows us to do what other animals cannot: read the interior states of others of our kind. To survive, we need to know our own inner state and those of others, quickly, at a glance, deeply."

--From *Programming the Posthuman* by Ellen Ullman.

In the Animal Kingdom

I sit here now as I sat here then. He's not here now; he wasn't here then. The only difference between now and then—fifteen years ago—is that I know the difference.

Then? Then, I had a child's imagination, a child's belief that all things were possible—even the impossible—perhaps because I had no knowledge of *im*. *Im* is a prefix that comes with age, with experience, with rejection and failure. Slowly. More quickly if you have nothing worth rejecting. Then, *im* comes at you without mercy. And very quickly, you can no longer even see the word "possible" without its attendant *im*.

But that was fifteen years ago—when I was a mere child—with a child's imagination, a child's belief, and a child's still imperfect vision. None of which could really distinguish between *im* and *him*. And *him* was what I'd been anticipating for almost a whole year.

Today, the greatest of all days on the American calendar, is Thanksgiving—now as then. No other holiday—he'd said it himself many times—can compare. It's the day on which we all come home, wherever home may be. Sometimes, that home is just a heartbeat. But so long as a heart is beating, it yearns for home. And home is what we come to—on Thanksgiving.

"What time is Papa coming?" I shout from where I'm sitting next to the front window.

"Six o'clock," my mother shouts back from the kitchen.

"And if he *doesn't*?" I ask.

"He'll be here. We agreed. And if there's one thing your father *is*, it's punctual."

To myself, I think: I know. It's the German in him. He can't help himself *or* being punctual—whatever "punctual" means.

"It's the German in him," my mother shouts, unprompted. "He can't help himself."

My sister looks at me. I look back at her. We've both heard the words many times before. At a quarter to six on a cold and wet November afternoon, there's little comfort—dry *or* warm—in hearing this same old harangue about my father and *his* people.

Her Russia and *his* Germany—I realize now—were thousands of miles apart and two generations distant. Nevertheless, the ethnic slurs they exchanged had always begun like swift after-kicks on the hoof of an argument: a land-grab here, a *pogrom* there, *Gestapo* tactics everywhere. Not to mention any number of other "old Europe" defects that lodged in their genes and coursed through their veins—and so through my sister's and mine—like slightly flawed diamonds on an otherwise steady stream of pure Doodle Dandy lava.

This was the first Thanksgiving since their separation, which my father liked to call "collateral damage" by way of association with that other undoing in lower Manhattan. But the real truth of *their* undoing was another matter altogether.

"What time is it *now*, Mama?" I yell out again from my perch where Alice and I sit like a couple of famished baby birds.

"5:57. Any minute now. Trust me. No, don't trust *me*. Trust *him*."

I put my cheek up against the window and close my eyes tight. And *that's* when I begin to see him . . .

He's wearing an old, black corduroy coat, which I recognize immediately, and which I'd once seen hanging on a throwaway hanger in the basement. I asked my mother about it at the time, and she told me it had been my father's coat from his college days—something he'd picked up at a thrift shop for a couple of bucks, and which he'd too often and too proudly called his "Diogenes coat."

"So why does he keep it?" I asked.

"I dunno. Maybe he thinks he'll need it again one day. There are many things about your father I don't understand." With that, the conversation ended, and we both promptly forgot about the coat—until now.

As he comes up the street, I look more closely at this coat. It's ragged, worn gray in spots where it should be black, the collar too wide, the sleeves too short.

As he moves closer, I notice he's carrying a bag—a dark, brown plastic bag. I know my father and I know that bag. The contents of a dark brown plastic bag can be only one thing. This is, after all, Thanksgiving—the greatest feast of the year.

He steps up and rings the bell. Alice and I run to answer.

When I open the front door, my first impression is that he's aged. Maybe it's the coat, I decide. That, or something about his hair. My father had always been careful about his hair, especially in times of economic recession. "Good times might come and go," he'd chuckle. "But my hairline takes the longer view and stays the course," he'd invariably add with a flair for the obvious. This time, however, I'm so sure that his coat—or his hairline, for that matter—are holding fast to any course whatsoever.

It's merely a first impression. We fling the door open, and he scoops us both up while managing very carefully, I notice, to keep the contents of the brown plastic bag out of harm's way.

He brings the three of us inside—me, Alice and the bag—to greet my mother, who comes out of the kitchen bearing a dish towel like a Jersey barrier. This isn't their first meeting since the separation. But this is their first on a significant holiday. In other words, this is their first *contractual* meeting.

My mother looks down at the bag. "Happy Thanksgiving," she says in a guarded monotone.

"*Ditto*," my father offers in return. (My father has always believed in brains over brawn. And, whenever possible, he uses Latin to prove it.) He quickly diverts his glance from my mother to the dining table, puts both Alice and me down before seating himself, then holds the bag up to her as if surrendering a weapon.

"It looks fabulous! Here," he says. "The red's for the turkey. The white is for everything that comes up between now and the delectation of that turkey."

"We're having goose," my mother says.

"Ah," my father says, not even trying to conceal the fact of his pleasure. "*Goose!* We haven't had goose since our very own first Thanksgiving together. Before these little munchkins—." The last of his declaration goes the way of former Thanksgiving goose dinners, unknown to both Alice and me. "'Must be a special occasion," he deadpans—an all-too-familiar smirk forming at the corners of his mouth.

Alice and I look at each other. We've just spent a whole week preparing for such a contingency. If my father can have his collateral damage—we reasoned—we can have our preëmptive strike.

I harrumph, and my father looks at me. I indicate with my eyes a sign, taped to the wall directly behind his head. He turns around and reads.

HUMOR ENJOYS THE SAUCE OF SARCASM ABOUT AS MUCH AS A LIVE TURKEY ENJOYS THE THOUGHT OF ITS STUFFING

My father turns back and stares at me. I know his angry stare, and this isn't it. Instead, there's just a hint of appreciation in his eyes—the kind I was once used to seeing whenever Alice or I might say something that struck him as truly amusing.

It's a look of appreciation that never failed to produce in me the same sensation I'd once felt whenever he'd put his arm around me and call me his guy. It's the same sensation I felt whenever I'd performed well at some sport, and would then look in his direction for a reaction. He wouldn't shout or rave like other parents. He'd just give me a firm, quiet thumbs-up. Whatever I might've just accomplished on a given field or court or diamond, however loud the cheers or rants of other kids' parents, I'd look for that thumb. When I found it, I always felt that kind of shudder which opens like a gasp, closes like a sigh.

"Goose," he says, looking at my mother. "I can hardly wait!" He then looks at Alice and me and winks. I wink back, now feeling supremely confident about Alice's and my first success as peacemakers.

My mother returns to the kitchen. My father sits down in the Mission Style armchair we inherited as part of their separation agreement— *his* chair, once, but which he'd given up without a fight. He runs his hands along the arms of that chair as I'd seen him run his hands many times along my mother's arms. Abruptly, he glances away, but only for an instant. His eyes and thoughts then return once again to us and to the occasion—and, his arms outspread, Alice and I rush in.

"Thanksgiving. Who amongst you can tell me the story of Squanto and the first Thanksgiving?" he asks with *faux* ceremony.

"Who *between* you, you mean," I correct. "There are only two of us here." He gives me another one of his looks—doubtless piqued by my correction, but awed, too, by this bit of erudition I'm showing off like a pair of shiny new silver spurs.

"Okay, who between you? And who *between* you is going to cast the *next* stone?"

"Fowler says—," I start in, careful, as he always used to insist, to know and quote my sources accurately.

"Fowler said many things," he interrupts. "But Fowler's dead, and dead men don't cast stones. Who *between* you can tell me something about Squanto?"

I know, of course, because he brought the story to my attention years ago. Alice is too young to know the answer—or rather, to understand the *real* question. He isn't asking whether one of us knows the story of Squanto and the first Thanksgiving. No, he's asking whether either of us remembers how we came to know the story.

I pause. At this moment, I understand, perhaps for the first time, how important it is to my father to be remembered and appreciated—as a father, as a provider, as a teacher—at least by his own children.

For months now, he's been on the outside looking in. Our contact has been almost exclusively by telephone. He's been out there somewhere, at a distance, and growing more distant and detached by the day. But he still has an urgent need to instruct. He still wants to believe that his accumulated knowledge of the way things work, however skewed, is of some value—if only to us. He still wants to believe that if he can't directly feed us, clothe us, put a roof over our heads, he can at least give us a leg up on the world in which he, himself, has so badly stumbled.

"Squanto," I begin, "was an Indian, sold into slavery in Spain."

My father gives me an encouraging nod. "That's him. *He's* the one."

Now it's my turn to sigh and stare back at my father. "Squanto was about hurt and separation and the pain of loneliness. Squanto was also about forgiveness. And about more hurt, separation and loneliness. But also about more forgiveness. I don't know whether Squanto was a real person or only a symbol."

"You mean *personification*?" my father shoots back—too quickly and recklessly it seems to me. Yet I can see in his eyes—whatever refinement he needs to supply to my symbol—that he's immensely pleased with my characterization of Squanto and with my understanding of the subtext of the story.

There's something I catch in his eyes for the first time, and I wince inwardly as I see it. On the one hand, I feel the pleasure of my understanding; on the other, I feel a fear of something until now quite unfamiliar. What I see in my father's eyes is his own pain—or at least the appearance of pain.

Sure, I know what real pain is, and that it often results in tears. I've seen tears of pain, almost daily, on Alice's cheeks. I know the occasional feeling of tears on my own cheeks, though less often now that I'm getting older and am not supposed to cry over every little scratch or unkind word. I even knew what tears look like on an adult's cheeks, as I've seen many such adult cheeks in the weeks and months since the undoing. And, of course, I've seen tears on my mother's cheeks since my parents' separation—though only in the kitchen and only whenever she thought she was alone. Even then, she's always seemed to meet my stare from around the corner with an onion in one hand and a knife in the other, as if to dismiss each new eruption of tears as the collusion of a silly vegetable and of a knife's untimely cutting of it.

I notice that Alice is fidgeting. But I want to pursue this new knowledge, and decide to try a different tact just to see if it might produce a different reaction.

"I was looking at the moon last night," I say. "At the *man* in the moon." The leather of his chair creaks as my father leans forward. "Sometimes, I'd look away. Then I'd look back again. Other times, I'd just blink. And each time I looked again, the man in the moon had a different expression. Sometimes he looked happy, sometimes, sad—or surprised, or disappointed, or even confused. The more I looked at his eyes, the more wrinkly they got—mostly, around his left eye. It looked like he had a black eye, or maybe a scar. Do you suppose he was ever a boxer?" I finally ask with what I know even now to be a stab at something adults call irony.

My father smiles at this second exhibition of my shiny new spurs.

"Cosmic debris," he mutters. "The man in the moon is always boxing with cosmic debris."

I look at him in complete confusion and think for a moment he might be speaking French—as he sometimes would on holidays.

"It's the stuff that flies through the night—the stuff you can never anticipate. That even the man in the moon can't anticipate, and so he just takes it on the chin. You can't plan for it. You can't build a defense against it. It just happens."

I continue to look at him and wonder when I might finally be allowed to resume.

"Sorry," he says. "Just rambling. Go on."

"What I wanted to ask," I start in again, "is why the man in the moon always seems to be changing his expression."

My father looks at me and begins to squeeze his chin as if it were half a lemon. What I'd seen earlier in his eyes is now gone as he struggles to find his fatherly voice of authority. Finally, and entirely out of character, he says "I dunno. But maybe we can work on a theory. Whaddya say?" he now asks with an ad hoc Brooklyn accent I know to be pure phony-bologna, and which causes me to shudder.

We are, thankfully, saved by my mother's announcement of dinner. "Soup's on," she shouts from the kitchen.

Alice and I take our places at the table. My father, of course, is already sitting, and the three of us now turn our attention to the real reason this is the greatest of all days on the American calendar.

On one side of the table stand various *zakuski*; on the other, *Vorspeisen*. In between, like a happy Maginot Line—and every bit as porous—stand two bottles of French wine, one red and one white, a pepper mill and candelabrum. We can choose—if little hands care to pass through that line like intrepid soldiers—from the one side: *Rotkohl*; *Sauerkraut*; plain, unadorned herring; asparagus wrapped in Westphalian ham; coleslaw with walnuts and raisins; thinly sliced pieces of *Kasslerrippchen*. From the other side: sturgeon caviar and salmon roe; smoked pike and whitefish; *selyodka* swimming in waves of oil and vinegar with little onions like whitecaps; also *maslo* and *pashtet iz seldi*; *pirozhki*; *vinegret*; and an assortment of other salads.

In my view, the Russians clearly have the advantage. And yet, in an effort at culinary *détente*—my mother's transparent attempt at a Molotov-Ribbentrop treaty—lie side by side and on one plate what she calls *Buterbrodi* and what my father calls *Butterbrötchen*. Her version, with red caviar looking like tiny red balloons; his, with plain butter—each slice standing like a smart little ship with a creamy golden delicacy in its cargo.

Our feast—no word sums it up more succinctly—is saluting from atop white lace covering ecru-colored holiday linen (all of which I now understand, fifteen years later, to have been left over from a previous era in which my parents had conclusively disposed of a sizably disposable income).

My father stands up, reaches for the bottle of white wine, and walks to my mother's end of the table.

"*Du vin blanc, Madame?*" he asks like the princely student-waiter he'd once been.

"*Mais oui, bien sûr, Monsieur,*" my mother aspirates to complete her part in the ceremony.

He fills her glass to three-quarters.

"*Spasibo*," she says laconically to an alienated husband who's once again courting her in the guise of a charming student-waiter.

"*Bitte*," he answers, reduced to a single Teutonic sound bite.

He walks back to his end of the table and fills his own glass. Alice and I also have wine glasses for the occasion, though they cater only to apple juice.

From a standing position, my father raises his glass. "*Zu den Abwesenden*," he announces grandly. "*Za otsyustvyuskikh*," my mother pronounces as if from under the dark clouds of Eastern Europe, and so with far less of my father's sunny Western disposition. Then, for our benefit — though we already know both expressions by sound — they pronounce in unison: "To the absent ones."

After a few seconds' pause, and with utensils now busily in motion, my mother continues. "You're looking well. Well, if also a little thin."

"*Qui dort, dîne*," my father mutters. And then, to the two of us, "As the French would say, 'He who sleeps, eats.' In addition to which, I've joined — rather, *rejoined* — the School of Peripatetics," he announces.

A moment of silence lies sodden before my mother breaks it. "For the children's benefit, what exactly is the School of Peripatetics?"

My father settles his knife and fork quietly back down on his dinner plate as his eyes and the corners of his mouth run to take up battle-stations behind a smirk. He knows that this "for the children's benefit" is nonsense. I know that he knows it. He knows that I — and maybe even my mother — know it. Only Alice is still too young to share in the general family omniscience. As amusing as it might be in certain other word games we play, in this instance it is not. In fact, it has become one of our unhappier routines whenever we find ourselves seated at the dinner table.

I seek to quash it before it can erupt yet again into tension and closed mouths. I nod at another of Alice's and my creations on the wall, this one hanging directly over the hutch with an illustration of a very fat, very satisfied cat. My father looks and reads soundlessly:

SMIRKS ARE UNBECOMING, UNLESS ON A CHESHIRE CAT

"Very clever," my father says — but with nothing like the enthusiasm he'd shown upon reading our first billboard.

In the same instant, he disengages the muscles that hold the smirk, finds a couple of vagrants to replace it with a scowl, and continues in earnest to Alice and me. "Peripatesis was the brainchild of Socrates, who didn't like to write. Its effectiveness was noted by Plato—and to some laughable degree also by Xenophon—who had to walk and write at the same time because Socrates couldn't be bothered. This was all later documented and codified by Plato's greatest pupil, Aristotle—born a full fifteen years after Socrates' death—who believed that people absorbed and assimilated— *learned*, if you will—new information better if they were in motion, even if just walking while talking." He leans back again and picks up his knife and fork, a signal to us that he's ready for summation. "And so, it was really about walking and talking and doing. Which is why, to this day—."

My father's eyes rather too cavalierly move to my mother's end of the table—then, however, pull up short as they meet not an appreciative smile, but a yawn.

I know it's entirely unintentional. I'm sure he does, too. And yet, nothing in her arsenal can turn him from gregarious to taciturn more quickly and more soundlessly than a yawn. His own radar can spot a yawn—particularly one of my mother's—and all of his defenses go on foolish, full-scale alert. To his credit, perhaps, even *he* can appreciate that not everyone shares his enthusiasm for things like "peripatesis."

I try to get him back on topic. "Which is why, to this day—?" I repeat, but he won't be distracted. He simply returns to his dinner. The discussion—his holding forth, really—is now finished, and nothing, not even one of Alice's and my billboards, can return us to the holiday mood of just seconds earlier.

For once, my father doesn't say anything disparaging, and my mother doesn't pretend to excuse herself. We're at a standstill. It feels like old times, and old times don't feel so good—especially at Thanksgiving. We chew and swallow, each in his or her own way, each pretending that the happy sounds of holiday cheer still prevail over the near silence of chewing and swallowing.

Alice and I have worked on other billboards. They all hang there, just waiting like Band-Aids for blisters to break out from some ill-timed word from him, some yawn from her. But our remaining billboards have already become redundant and, like my father, will find no further employ. The silence, deeper than any blister, persists. Alice and I look up at each other from time to time—and for once, no giggle crosses either of our minds.

I glance at my father out of the corner of my eye. His face looks strained, much older than even just an hour ago, and minus any remnant of the appreciation of my erudition or of Alice's and my wit. He, too, simply eats.

Our plates are almost empty. A single piece of goose remains on the platter. My father and I are now approaching that point at which we'll often stage a mock standoff, when both of us are still hungry—or at least pretending to be hungry. This contest of wills and appetite is one I've grown used to, grown fond of, grown up with as a rite of passage and as something my father likes to call "atavistic." He has tried to explain it to me on a few occasions, but "atavistic" has, each time, gone the way of "peripatetic."

It has always been my father's contention that the reigning male of a pride or pack gets the first spoils of a hunt, can eat his fill, and will only *then* allow his mate and cubs to gorge themselves on the remaining bits. This—once again, according to my father—is nature's law. He always illustrates it, his own fork poised with slightly menacing tines, over the last bit of meat or other desired edible. At this same moment, with weapon hovering, he'll utter the injunction "In the animal kingdom. . ." leaving the rest of the explanation to flutter off like some elliptical butterfly.

However much I might pretend to challenge his claim, he never fails to remind me of the law of the jungle. If he then grants me this last remainder, it's only to sit back in his chair with the benign smile of one who has just bestowed a favor upon a subordinate. This, he knows, is *also* the law of the jungle—but of the *human* jungle.

I time my last mouthful to coincide with *his* last while keeping my fork aloft and with the tines pointed in the direction of the meat platter and of that single drumstick. My only competitor for the remaining bit ignores my challenge and continues to chew, holding his own spear nonchalantly. At last he swallows, and I see his eyes focus on the platter that lies before us. As he raises his arm and spear in its direction, I quickly move my own arm and spear towards the same target-fowl. Our tines pierce the flesh simultaneously, and I look hard into his face in happy anticipation of the commencement of our ritual.

In the brief seconds that pass between his silent stare and mine, I see his eyes, like those of the man in the moon, pass rapidly through phases and moods to settle finally on the one I'd seen earlier in the afternoon.

I jab at the drumstick so as to prod him on to a challenge. He doesn't respond. Instead, he slowly withdraws his fork.

Please, Papa, no! I think to myself—and yet, for once I hope he can read my mind—"quickly, at a glance, deeply." Fight for it! It's yours. You're still king. Please, Papa. Fight me for it!

But he simply retires his fork and aligns it noiselessly alongside his knife.

I now *open* my eyes—my cheek still pressed hard against the front window, my father nowhere in sight. The street is dark. It would now be well past six o'clock. Alice is on the floor playing with the only set of toys she hasn't yet broken without hope of replacement: her ten fingers. My mother comes out of the kitchen and announces dinner. I stand up from the couch and take my place opposite hers—where, I imagine, my father would sit if he were here.

My mother lights a single votive candle in the center of the table. She serves both Alice and me a hefty portion of chicken nuggets onto which she grates a bit of nutmeg. I notice she's bought ketchup for the occasion—a holiday treat. For herself, she's prepared a single chicken breast and a spoonful of rice, no nutmeg.

She drinks water. The two of us drink apple juice. We all drink out of water glasses.

"Happy Thanksgiving," she says as she raises her glass of water and, with her eyes, implores us to do the same.

"Happy Thanksgiving," we answer in unison as we raise our glasses of apple juice. I look hard at my mother, but Alice—I notice out of the corner of my eye—doesn't look up from her plate.

We eat. The only sound in the room is that of three people eating and swallowing—and digesting the absence of a fourth. I understand. Certain buildings have come undone, and families have come undone with them. The once proud circumstances of a disposable income and of a fine roof over a foursome of heads have changed, and it is only fit that we change with them. Under this newer roof, and with only my mother's income to keep it attached, goose is no longer on the menu. Nuggets are. But *we*, at least, have nuggets and a roof. For that, we can be thankful at Thanksgiving—the one, *true* celebration.

I stand up and raise my glass. I look first at Mama, then at Alice. "*Zu den Abwesenden*," I say. "To the absent ones," they say in unison—neither of them raising their eyes from the table.

Something Special

A Novella

Chapter ONE

"Brucie, I need work," she whines.

She says this, mind you, as she reaches out and begins to toggle a long, manicured fingernail back and forth against a small lump of something stuck to the square of my desk calendar. I glance down; see that it's stuck to a smaller square of blank white space; see that it's the only thing residing on that small square other than the print of today's date. The grating of her fingernail—never mind the gesture—makes me want to do the same with my teeth, but I squelch the urge.

"Yes, I know. We *all* need work, Angie. It's what keeps us happy, healthy, not housebound." I'd like to think I have a way with words.

"Well?"

"Well, Angie, you know there's always that *one* thing you can do—."

She raises an eyebrow but not her glance from that lump of something brown and unsightly stuck to my calendar. I decide it must be a remnant of yesterday's lunch—left over from a week earlier and feeding on its own ration of MSG in a small refrigerator I keep humming above the supply closet in the far corner of my office. That same closet is home to a combination copier and fax machine. Times are tough all around.

"Well, don't blame *me* for your situation!" I say. "You don't want to wait tables, cashier or coat-check. You can't type, can't file, can't even manage the phone if it has more than one line. You can't spell worth a damn — you've said so yourself. And you've never even tried to balance a checkbook. What do girls like you do if they don't do that *other* thing?"

Her eyebrow does an encore.

"You can't milk cows here in New York, Angie. We don't have cows except on milk cartons." I pull, as if in reflection, on my earlobe. "You could get *yourself* on a milk carton, you know, but you'd have to go reported as missing. I suppose I could help with that, but we'd first have to figure out my percentage. It's not my usual line of work."

"If you were doing your usual line of work, Brucie, I wouldn't be here right now. I'd be out doing shoots — runway, catalogue, covers."

"Angie, *Angie,* you're not a cover kinda girl. You're a Holstei—, wholesome kinda girl. Ya know, farm-bred. Healthy. Robust. Girl next door. Or at least the girl next farm."

"Not funny, Brucie."

"It's the wrong season for catalogues," I say, now a little tired of toying with her. She's said "Brucie" three times in the space of thirty seconds, and it's beginning to annoy me. She's taking liberties, god*damn* it. If there'd been some give in our relationship — as there's been with my other girls — then I certainly wouldn't mind a bit of take. But there's been none. She's all take and no give, and I'm getting annoyed.

The problem is simple: I want something from her and she knows it. What's more, we both know *exactly* what it is I want, and she seems to enjoy making that "something" increasingly difficult to get.

"I'm not going that route, Brucie, so forget it. I didn't work this hard and come all this way just to do what I coulda done in Iowa at twice the price and a third the cost."

I wonder about her math, about her understanding of the local supply-and-demand, about her knowledge of her own market worth. Also about how "hard" she's worked to get to where she is and about how "hard" it was to grab a Greyhound from somewhere just nowhere south of Des Moines all the way to Port Authority. Yeah, sure, she also managed to find her way to my office on the eighty-fifth floor of the Empire State Building, and that's worth something. But so have lots of other girls. And those girls have also managed to show something like gratitude, admiration even — if not for me directly, at least for the view. This one hasn't shown anything but attitude.

"Fine by me, Angie."

"Fine by *you,* Brucie," she says with a sneer, still single-mindedly sticking it to the thing stuck to my desk calendar.

We sit in silence a moment as she continues to work at the lump.

Finally, she gets it unstuck; cranes her neck forward; lets go with a little gust of wind. The lump lands in the pleat of my trousers, and I immediately brush it to the floor. The clock on my wall chimes twelve. Lunch, I think.

"Whaddya say we go get something to eat?" I ask. Ordinarily, a little lunch with vino might lead to a little something else. Where Angie's concerned, however, hope's a bicycle with no chain.

"*Fabulous* idea!" she says with what I take to be genuine appreciation. "Sit-down lunch?"

"Sure, why not?"

"Someplace with a tablecloth and silver?"

"The works."

"Bruce, you're an angel! Let me just go powder my nose."

I understand the expression to be part of her arsenal — like the raised eyebrow. Both quite quaint. I reach into my desk drawer and pull out the key to the ladies' room, push it across the desk and let my finger remain an instant alongside hers. She doesn't withdraw immediately, and I think — . But no, this is Angie I remind myself — and the brief mingle of our fingers is, I know, about as much as I can expect for my offer of a free lunch.

While she's doing whatever she does in the ladies', I make a quick calculation. There's a sit-down diner a few blocks away whose specialty is quick, relatively clean, and very cheap. Aspiring cover girl that she is, she'll make do with a salad. I'll be out a coupla bucks, but I don't mind parting with the cash when I consider that I'll have her all to myself to think about in those special ways I like to think about my girls.

She returns and hands back the restroom key. I step around from my desk, help her into her winter coat, admire the way her chest heaves forward as she reaches back to find a sleeve. That the top three buttons of her blouse are unbuttoned doesn't exactly vitiate the view.

We leave my office and call an elevator. There are a number to choose from at this level, so our wait — in silence — is short. I stand close enough to Angie to admire the scent.

"What's that you're wearing?" I ask as I crinkle my nose in the air.

"'Come Hither'," she deadpans.

"Oh. Don't mind if I do," I say — but the smartness of my jest is lost to the excitement of the elevator doors now opening.

Once outside Empire, she seems quite bubbly and eases right into the pedestrian flow. I, myself, normally hate the jostle of bodies on the street. But in this instance, I find I don't mind at all if a straggler forces me to bump up against one of Angie's softer parts. She's apparently so intent on finding a restaurant *de luxe*, she doesn't even seem to notice an occasionally errant elbow — namely mine. In the meantime, I steer her west past Schwab Brokerage Services and Empire Erotica, then finally through the door of the Cheyenne Diner at the corner of 33rd Street and 9th Avenue. So New York, I think to myself. Money, sex, food — all cheek by jowl.

"Hallo – ?" is only halfway off her lips when a steamroller of a woman in standard hostess black grabs two menus and scoots us both to a booth. Angie sits; the eyebrow rises.

"You'll *love* the selection," I say to her before she has an opportunity to object, then sink down out of sight behind the two enormous leaves of my menu. She won't, of course, but that's a little beside the point.

After a couple of minutes, I peek out over the top of my menu to see where she's headed on the page. I'm not just a little piqued when I realize she's eyeing the $23.95 prime rib with what I suspect is a vengeance. If my heart wants to believe the rigor of her stare is an attempt at concentration, the cold and calculated glint in her eye tells me otherwise.

At this moment, however, some comic relief appears in the form of a waiter. I know I'm looking at one of Manhattan's myriad of wannabe actors — too pretty to be waiting tables except between gigs when the rent has to be paid and when crating lunch to Manhattan's millions of hungry mouths is the easiest way to do it. Angie looks up, all cuteness and smiles.

"Hi!" he says.

"Hi!" she says.

"What'll you have today?" he asks her and her only, and I wonder whether this moron has any idea who'll be paying the tab and leaving the tip.

"I believe I'll just have a small salad. Lemon wedge on the side if you wouldn't mind."

"A big healthy girl like you, just a salad?" he asks, and I immediately want to suggest they get a room or at least take it out to the sidewalk.

"Well, I'm sure *you* know how it is," she says. The reciprocal ogling and appraising of bumps and curves is beginning to make me car-sick.

"You're not interested in a steak, Angie?" I ask. "A big, healthy girl like you?"

She ignores me, though the tell-all eyebrow is clearly itching to rise up and tell me where to get off. "And a glass of water, please — " she cranes her head up and over to read his name-plate, curiosity now buzzing in the buttercup of her cuteness " — Randall."

He smiles down at her — big grin revealing "Made in U.S.A." dental hygiene that would make klieg lights cringe.

"Is that your stage name or your real name?" Angie asks.

"*Comme vous voulez*," he says with a wink — and I think I actually make a retching sound.

Randall *garçon* or Randall *acteur* is already retiring his notepad to his rear pocket and picking up our menus when I have to stay his thespian's hand. "Would it be too much to ask you to take *my* order as well?"

"Oh, so sorry!" he says with an embarrassed laugh — then looks immediately at Angie as if to ask for animal comfort.

"Don't worry, Randall. That sort of thing happens all the time to Brucie," she says as she reaches out to touch his arm and return the wink.

"I'd like a pastrami on rye, toasted, with a side of cole slaw."

"Something to drink?"

"Iced tea. Unsweetened."

"I understand," he says. "You bring your sugar with you," he adds as he – God help me! — smiles down at Angie once again.

I suddenly feel as if I've been yanked out of time and place and dropped into a truck stop eatery somewhere in the Midwest, so banal and predictable is their palaver. Now, I'm *really* annoyed. "Yes," I say. "And I'm the daddy."

Randall's mouth-work is like the kind of warm-up exercises I imagine actors or radio announcers have to do just before they step out onto the stage or in front of a microphone. He's clearly lost in how to interpret my quip — never mind how to respond to it — and I think, only briefly, *how sad*.

"That was mean," Angie says just as soon as Randall is out of earshot.

"Not in the least," I answer. "He's a waiter. He should remember his station."

"He's an *actor*," she instructs.

"Whatever," I sling back at her — an expression I've grown to hate since it was first hijacked by her generation of language hooligans. But I occasionally like a bit of street-fighting myself, and this one word can take on gangs.

We sit in silence until Randall reappears several minutes later with lunch. My rye bread has only seen the reflection of a toaster — I can see that at a glance — but Angie's salad is the picture of a Penjing garden. He actually delivers her lemon — two halves with the rinds curly-cued and pointing off towards some unseen Buddha — on a separate plate atop a translucent doily. How do I know the doily's translucent? Because the moron has slipped a piece of paper underneath with — I'm quite certain, even if reading upside down and backwards is a bit of a challenge—his name and telephone number scribbled out with theatrical flourish.

"Anything else I can bring you?" he asks, looking only at Angie.

"Not for the moment," I answer for her.

Angie smiles meekly—or is it sweetly—I can no longer distinguish.

We eat in silence until I grow weary of it.

"Angie, I'm planning to go out to California week after next. I've got business there." For all the enthusiasm she shows, I might've announced a fire drill. "I'm thinking of spending a night or two in Yosemite National Park. Have you ever been?"

"No."

"It's really one of the wonders of the world," I say, trying to conjure up a note of excitement for natural landscapes I've frankly never felt except when those landscapes were flesh-colored, young, firm and feminine. "By the way" —I add almost cavalierly— "I'll be staying at the Ahwahnee Hotel. Ever heard of it?"

"No."

"It's considered best of class—the watering-hole of many famous people when they just want to get away from it all. Tycoons, magnates. Celebrities, actors."

"Uh-huh," she drawls—although I register a slight uptick in her interest at my mention of actors and celebrities.

"Yes. And I thought I might take one of my more promising *protégées* with me. It'd be something special."

"Really? Something *special*." She turns a smile on me just like the one she'd turned on Randall moments earlier, and I sense a small window of opportunity. "Would I have to audition for the part?" she asks—and for the first time ever in Angie's case, I discern wit.

"You may've noticed, Angie—my office lacks a casting couch."

"Whew! For a moment there, I was thinking I might actually have to take something off."

"Just the scowl, Angie. Randall and I, we like you much better when you're smiling."

"Would I get my own room in the Ah—. Wha'd you say the name of the hotel was again?"

"The Ahwahnee. And the answer's 'no.' Do you have *any* idea what their rooms cost a night?"

"Nope. But that's not really my problem, is it."

"They cost a fortune."

"Oh. But I'm worth it, right?" she says with a smile that is at once disarming, almost flirtatious.

"You *may* be."

"Why do you want to bring me along, Bruce?" she asks. I actually rather like the presumptiveness in her question. She asked for the job on the spot; by God, I'll give it to her.

"I think we can work on your book. Your headshots are fine, but you need some full-body shots."

The eyebrow shoots up once again. "Oh? So, like, you're suddenly both my agent *and* my photographer?"

"I know how to handle a camera. And I've been around models for a long time. It's my profession. My intent here is professional, Angie. Purely professional."

"And your full-body shots? What's with that?"

"Look at what *Sports Illustrated* has done for its swimsuit models. Consider the possibilities."

This time, it's neither a scowl nor a smile she flashes back at me, but a cold stare. "I don't take my clothes off for *anybody*, Brucie."

I ignore the "Brucie." "Look, I've read about this place called Mirror Lake. We can walk to it from the hotel. From what I've read, you couldn't ask for a better backdrop. We'll just put you there on a rock like the Little Mermaid — you know, the nymphet look." I realize as soon as it's out of my mouth that I've said the wrong thing. "Nymph-anything" is not a description Angie's likely to develop a fondness for.

"I don't take my clothes off for a picture, Brucie. I don't care *what* the scenery is."

"Okay, okay. You can wear a bodysuit. We'll shoot at sunset, and no one will know the difference."

"Uh-huh."

This part of the negotiation is apparently at an end. And yet, if I think I've won my way at least into Angie's heart, I'm mistaken.

"Do I at least get my own bed?" she asks.

"Sure, no problem," I say as I make a mental note to reserve the honeymoon suite — cost be damned.

"Cool!" she almost explodes. "My first road-trip as a professional model!"

"Then we're agreed?" I ask just to confirm our deal.

"We are, Bruce. I can hardly wait!"

"Why don't you run right out and buy yourself a nice, new, flesh-colored bodysuit. Try the dance supply places up around Lincoln Center." She purses her lips in a way that lets me know her cash-flow is tight — that I might have to do a bit of provisioning. I sigh, then reach for my wallet. "Of course, we could save the money and just suit you up for your birthday on that rock."

"Huh?"

"Never mind," I say as I pull out three twenties.

"Why, thank you, Bruce," she says as she reaches across the table and snatches the bills out of my hand. "I'll be sure to bring back a receipt and your change."

"I'm sure you will, Angie. Now just run along, will you, while I take care of the bill."

She smiles again and slides out of the booth. I notice that she has neglected — or forgotten — to take the slip of paper out from under the doily. As I watch her exquisite backside move off down the aisle and towards the exit, I consider some of the perqs of this job — curve-watching being among the most demanding in time and attention. But watching is not doing, I reflect — knowing now that it's only a question of time.

Chapter TWO

Not even two weeks later, I'm sitting next to Angie as we begin our decent into San Francisco's international airport. She snores like a marmot, her head wedged in between the headrest and the window and about as far away from mine as she could possibly have put it. I might, of course, take advantage—but I'm no dentist; which is to say, I like mine alive, alert, fully conscious. Still, I can appreciate skylines as much as the next guy, and San Francisco's got a good one. I lean over Angie to look out the window, but get bogged down in the scenery most immediately below. My-oh-my... buttons have been popped in the eagerness, I suppose, of firm young lungs to breathe some California air. The view is breath-taking—yet not so overwhelming that I fail to notice once again her honeyed scent. The smell—dare I say?—is divine.

Angie snorts ever-so-gently. I quickly shift my glance to the window, but apparently not in time. She shrinks down and away, and her hand shoots up to cover her cleavage.

"We're about to land," I announce nonchalantly.

"Yes, Brucie, I see that." Her tone is not friendly, and I wonder what it is about a first view of San Francisco that gets some people so irked.

"Ya know, Angie, we could—either one of us—lose our hearts here."

Her face contorts. *"Huh?"*

I decide never again to remind her of our very different tastes in music, art, literature, botanica—any of which might lead to a discussion of our respective ages.

We eventually land, exit the plane, and make our way to the baggage claim area. Angie ogles other passengers, some of whom ogle in return—mostly young, male, rapacious. While we all stand around looking either anxious or supercilious as we mark the minutes waiting for a mammoth stainless steel dragon to disgorge its contents onto a conveyer belt, I note how she lends a quiet attention to one rather attractive female. The look on Angie's face—of which she is apparently entirely unaware as she inspects her competition—is storied. I wonder where she gets the breeding; or if this is simply the product of her days on the farm, at rodeos and state fairs, where hogs and steers might've stood stupidly by to be inspected for their fat/meat/sperm content.

When our bags finally arrive, she allows me to carry the lot as we make our way to the rental car area, process through, then walk out to pick up our vehicle. I've rented something sober rather than smart, as I'd like to discourage any show of that California road rage I've heard so much about. With Angie in the front seat, I hardly need to be driving something candy-apple red to bring on a shower of highway testosterone.

Within minutes, we're on the road and traveling east through some of the most rat's-ass boring country I've ever driven through. If this is California, I'm thinking, they can keep it. A brief two hours later, however, I'm practically struck dumb as we enter Yosemite National Park. I'm beginning to see what the proverbial fuss is all about and why people sometimes get misty-eyed when they talk about purple mountains' majesties. There's something here they may actually not be able to recreate in Manhattan—or even in Vegas. I'm half-expecting Angie to squiggle across out of pure joy and appreciation and let me put my arm around her. But when I glance over to see how she's taking it all in, I notice she's busy with her cuticles.

This girl-woman, I think to myself, is a case study in self-absorption—as narcissistic as a swan, a pond and no windy rival.

But then, I think, there's them tits.

After roughly an hour's travel over snow-splattered roads through forests full of trees that could tickle heaven with their tops, we arrive at something like civilization, and I'm almost thankful for the break in splendor. A road sign points the way to the Ahwahnee—and to no other hotel. I suspect we're in for some splendor of a man-made kind, and I'm wondering whether Angie's temperature is rising in spite of whatever signs of excitement she may *not* be showing.

When we arrive at the hotel entrance five minutes later, we're immediately greeted—and Angie's door is opened—by an attendant who asks whether he can take our luggage. Parting with even small change for a favor is not my forte, and I'm consequently thinking I'd like to bring our bags in and spare myself this tomfoolery of tipping. Angie, however, apparently has her mind set on inviting—and my paying for—red-carpet treatment.

"Oh, that would be lovely! Thank you *so* much for offering."

A second attendant appears outside my door, opens it, let's me step out and feel the soft crunch of designer gravel underfoot as I reach for my wallet and hope to God I've got a few singles handy. I do, slip him a pair, and let him climb in behind me while his buddy loads our luggage onto a mobile unit. Angie, meanwhile, is already halfway down a long corridor to the front entrance.

I actually have to jog to catch up to her—which I begrudgingly do. Before I can even begin to remonstrate, I see her expression: she's clearly delighted with her new surroundings; likes playing the princess bit; may just be in the mood to reciprocate if I don't put the clamps on too hastily. Instead of harsh words, I take her gently by the elbow and lead her to the front desk, where we're greeted warmly and effortlessly by a young lady whose nameplate reads "Meredith." I give her my name and credit card—and she responds with a courteous "We've been expecting you, Mr. And Mrs. Seymour. Welcome to the Ahwahnee." Fortunately, Angie doesn't protest the Missus bit.

Meredith processes the paperwork in short order and tells us our luggage will follow immediately, then gives me the room key and points out the location of the elevator. "If you're interested," she says, "high tea is now being served in The Great Lounge."

"Thank you, Miss. We shall certainly consider it," Angie says with an aplomb I suspect she can only just now have nipped, like some low-hanging rare fruit, from the Ahwahnee air.

As we exit the reception area and enter a huge room with logs blazing in a fireplace big as Mount Rushmore at one end, I can see from the reflected firelight in Angie's eyes that she's walking a tightrope between wanting to appear entirely at ease and allowing her excitement to shine through. The reception area and adjoining reading, lounging and dining rooms are indeed cavernous and on a scale I imagine no Manhattan hotel could afford, no Des Moines hotel could envision.

We're inside the elevator and on our way to the third floor, riding the shush of a warm mechanical wind. Only then does Angie look at me and exclaim, "It's *gorgeous!*"

"Yes, I thought you'd like it. The Queen of England apparently did, too," I add. "I don't know that she slept in *our* room, but we're breathing her same air."

"Recently?" Angie asks with an air of studied nonchalance.

"Well, actually, it was back in 1954. The Queen doesn't get out much."

The elevator comes to a vacuum-sealed stop and we get off. As I see directional signs on the wall in front of us and look again at our room key, the probability of a corner room already suggests itself—reinforcing, in turn, that my request of a bridal suite might've indeed been honored.

We walk down what must be one of the longest and quietest hotel corridors in Christendom until we come upon… the corner room. I open the door and Angie enters. I enter next. Stony silence brings up the rear.

I'm admiring—or at least looking curiously at—the Native American motif displayed in various instances throughout the room when Angie interrupts my inspection.

"I thought you promised me I'd have my own bed."

"Well, I did—" I manage to say as I look approvingly upon the king-size plot of sheets and pillows more regal than even *I'd* imagined at the time I made the reservation. I'm also pleased to see that someone has placed my special order of a dozen blood-red roses in a vase next to the bed. "Maybe there was a mix-up. I'm sure we can get a second bed in here, Angie. Why don't we just freshen up a bit and take a little walk out to Mirror Lake? It really is quite spectacular, you know, and the combination of natural beauty and crisp, clean mountain air might make you, uh, more receptive."

"Brucie, get on the phone right now. Get on the phone, call Meredith, and get a second bed in here—now." Angie is channeling Geronimo, arms tightly zigzagged across her chest, and I think how like the décor.

As I'm about to pick up the phone and have my dreams dashed into the bargain, a soft knock at the door announces the arrival of the porter with our luggage. I walk over and let him in, then give him a wide berth to do his duty. He lays out our bags while maintaining a pleasant stream of chatter in which he mentions my name at least four times. They train them well here, I think to myself. First-class. I pull my wallet out again, see that I'm out of singles, slide out a five-dollar bill because he's been so generous with my name, and extend it with the "5" in plain view. He actually bows his way out of the room.

"Why didn't you ask him for a second bed, Brucie? He was right here. He could've brought in a fold-out."

I have limited cards to play, but I have good ones. "It doesn't work that way with hotels like this, Angie. I've got to call the concierge to order a bed."

"Then call the goddamned concierge!"

"Angie, *Angie,* what's the rush? Let's go down and sit by the fire, have a cup of tea or two, then go for a walk. I'll notify the concierge, and he'll arrange to have it brought in while we're out of the room."

"Okay, but I want to see a second bed in here by the time we get back."

"Scout's honor."

We unpack our things, following which Angie slips into the bathroom to change clothes – though not without first locking the door. When she comes back out a couple of minutes later, it's in something like a summer dress, and I wonder about her sense of the season.

"Wild prints must be the new black," I say as the memory of a Bloomie's ad I'd recently seen tickles my mental funny bone. "It really is quite fetching." She craves a solid reason to smile, though I've given her only a slice of one. "But you know what they say: 'It ain't the clothes; it's the hanger.'"

This time, she really *does* smile—and I smile back. A truce at last, I think.

We take the elevator to the ground floor and walk into The Great Lounge. An elderly woman stands in front of a samovar at one end of the room taking orders in quiet tones and giving leisurely cups of tea in return. Customers then move on to what looks at a distance like a selection of pastries and cookies.

"Bruce, why don't you grab us a couple of armchairs in front of the fire, and I'll get us some tea." I'm stunned into silence by the suggestion of camaraderie that could almost pass for an overture. "Bruce? Tea?" she repeats.

"Sure. That'd be great."

"How do you take it?"

"Two lumps and cream if they've got some on hand."

Angie walks off in the direction of the samovar, and I make straight for the fireplace where I manage to secure space for two on a loveseat. When Angie returns a couple of moments later, she's carrying cargo: two cups of tea and a plate of something like *petits fours à la* Yosemite. She could at this moment be a French maid if only we had the apron, heels and mesh stockings.

She takes a seat next to me, and our knees actually touch. She doesn't withdraw, and I'm suddenly feeling more like the fire in front of us: all greedy and aflame for the running sap of her. She gives me my tea and offers the pastries. I note how, in preparing to sip from her own cup, her pinkie unfolds into space like the mechanical arm, in miniature, of some orbiting module moving out to full extension — reaching out to snatch a falling star, or at least to fix a nut or bolt on a second vehicle in distress. The finger hangs in the air like a festoon — what my British friends in the trade would call "posh toddy," even if only imitation toddy. I'm enchanted.

"Now about that walk —," I say.

"Oh, Bruce, *must* we? I feel like I'm in a castle. Can't we just stay here by the fire and watch the people come and go?"

"All talking of Michelangelo?" I ask, hanging a smirk.

We sit several more minutes in silence, and I watch Angie watching others. She's really quite a delight — and for all of my cynicism, I can't help falling a tiny bit in love with her. Or at least in well-meaning lust.

"It'll be dark in two more hours. We can get out to Mirror Lake with plenty of light to find our way back if we leave right now."

"I think — if you don't mind, that is — I'll just stay put. I'm a little tired from the trip, and would just like to relax."

I'm once again feeling the onset of annoyance, but I keep it to myself. "That's fine, Angie. I'll scout the route and the location so that when we go out tomorrow afternoon, we'll know exactly what we're looking for."

She reaches forward and lets her hand hover just above my knee. "You're a darling, Bruce."

Chapter THREE

I put on my hiking boots, get some advice and a map from Meredith at the front desk, and set out into the woods. The path—an old carriage road—is quite clearly marked for most of the way. Lack of observation or adequate light might get you easily lost—at which point there's no telling where you'd end up—but the trail is a well-trodden one, and a bit of attention to others' boot-prints leaves you in little doubt about your destination. Well over an hour later, I see a sign telling me I'm still .7 mile away from the lake, and I realize this hike represents something more than a comfy Sunday stroll. I may have to embellish a tad with Angie—not exactly a sportswoman from what I've seen—but the end will most assuredly justify the means.

My first view of water is no less stupefying than my first sight of the Redwoods and Sequoias as we entered the park. And yet, my sighting of what I believe to be the lake is in error; the spot I want is still a quarter of a mile off. I move on—and in the meanwhile, gaze occasionally up at what my map tells me are Mt. Watkins, Ahwiyah Point and Half Dome. The names have all the poetry of lentil soup, but the view can't be denied. I wonder only how it is that Christian missionaries didn't immediately throw down their crosses and go native when they first stood where I'm now standing.

When I finally find the spot I want at Mirror Lake, I learn there'd once been a turnstile here—so heavy was the traffic of ladies-in-waiting for a photograph. I can already see Angie through the lens I project with my cupped hands, and the composition is masterful. This trip may actually serve both our purposes, I think — and I'm genuinely happy that I can be her mentor.

By the time I get back, it's almost dark — and quite chilly. I shiver once as I hit the shade of the corridor leading up to the entrance, but am greeted by a blast of warm air the moment I open the door.

As earlier, logs ablaze at one end of The Great Lounge are warming the backsides of several hotel guests. I make my way immediately to the elevator, then to the third floor, then down the hall to our corner room.

When I open the door, it's to silence. There is — I quickly note — a fold-out bed now occupying the space between our king-size bed and the window, but Angie is nowhere in sight. I decide she's either gone out for a stroll or is off exploring other parts of the hotel. My sights, in any case, are now set on a shower.

I'm scrubbing away the stale bread crust feel of jet travel when I think I hear the door open. "Angie," I call. "Is that you?"

"It is."

"I thought maybe we'd lost you to the bears," I say with a chuckle.

"You didn't."

"I'll be out of here shortly, and then it's all yours."

"Okay. I'm in no hurry."

I get out moments later, shave and dry off, then decide I'll ask Angie for some clothes rather than make my rude appearance in a bath towel. I'm not as toned as I may've been five or six years ago, and I don't think I need to expose her tender eyes to the evidence.

"Angie, would you mind passing me my trousers and shirt through the door?"

I hear nothing, though detect motion. When she taps on the door a moment later, I open — and see a slightly ruffled version of the young lady I'd taken three hours earlier to tea.

"Thanks," I say as I reach for my clothes through the crack. I then dress and exit the bathroom. "All yours."

Half an hour later, she slips briefly out of the bathroom, goes to the closet and pulls something down — then returns to the bathroom, closes and locks the door.

Another twenty minutes later, she re-appears in a different dress — more subdued, more appropriate to late winter — and freshly made-up, and I have to admit the result leaves me speechless. If only I were fifteen years younger, I suspect we might now be engrossed in a very different kind of pre-prandial.

"You look stunning," I tell her.

"Thank you, Bruce."

We make our way downstairs and to the dining room, where a whole new set of visual gewgaws awaits us. The main dining hall is easily the length of three tennis courts end to end, and the width of two side by side. The ceiling is at a height I estimate to be over thirty feet, and is supported by stripped and polished pine logs. Wrought iron candelabras hang from those same pine timbers and are somehow complemented by additional candelabras on the tables. The look is medieval — yet in combination with the Native American motif of the hotel, I wonder whether the composite represents a teeth-grinding impasse reached between two different interior designers, or whether it's rather the result of one shareholder's hallucination in which chivalry and savagery came to blows for the same piece of hostelry.

In any case, I'm not left long to muse, as the maître-d' all but curtsies to take Angie by the arm — with me left wagging an obedient tail at their heels — and leads us to our table.

He seats us, smiles, and is replaced by a waiter who steps in with two menus. "Something to drink before dinner?" he asks.

"Angie?"

"I'd like a Long Island Iced Tea," she says, and I wonder whether the bartender will be able to find this one in his dusty *Old Mr. Boston.*

"Very good" — our waiter shows not the least sign of bemusement — "and for you, sir?"

"I'd like the wine list, please — and a glass of champagne."

"Excellent."

He pirouettes and is off. Next up is a busboy with a basketful of what are no doubt local, multi-grain, organically-grown products. I wonder for an instant whether Californians ever die — or just move on to another, higher plane or field of wheat, barley, oats, milk and honey. Angie demurs — no surprise — and I subsequently point at something I believe I can identify as bread-like.

Our waiter returns a moment later with drinks and a wine list. That we're not in a rush is something he intuits, I suppose, from long experience. "Just let me know when you're ready," he says, and I nod in gratitude for the privilege of one of modern life's greatest and rarest privileges: an unhurried meal.

Angie has apparently been studying the menu and is now quite unconsciously mouthing the names of some of the items I suspect exist only in the mind of the chef. I know that describing items on a dinner menu is just slightly less challenging than writing art, music or wine criticism: there are, after all, only so many ways you can embellish stew. Angie abruptly looks up from her menu with the expression of one seeking beatification.

"Bruce, what are 'calf's cheeks'?"

"I have *no* idea, Angie," I say—and for once it's true. If an Iowa farm girl can't identify which end of a farm pet has ended up here on the menu, I'm not about to try. Instead, I turn my attention to the wine list and decide to go locavore.

When our waiter wanders by our table a few minutes later, I give him a subtle signal that we're ready to order. I'm nothing if not pleasantly surprised when Angie orders the calf's cheeks with resolution. I opt for a much safer New York strip steak, then give him the bin number of a locally-grown Cabernet. He commits this information and a few additional details to short-term memory, then withdraws from our table with the order.

"That was very brave of you, young lady."

"Not really. I figure where cheeks are concerned, there's only one of two possibilities—and either way, they're gonna be soft."

"Good thinking," I say. "And if you find they're not to your liking, you can always have some of my steak."

Angie smiles at me just as the wine steward arrives with our bottle. I glance at the label and give him a nod. He cuts the cap, inserts the screw and withdraws the cork virtually in one smooth motion, then pours me a sip. I taste it, give him a second nod, and he pours both Angie and me a healthy portion.

We raise our glasses, and I look Angie in the eye. "To you," I say. "To you in the wilds of Yosemite."

"Lions and tigers and bears—and me!"

"Don't forget coyotes and wolves. Not to mention dodas and guibs."

"Oh, Bruce, this is a *park*, not a jungle."

"What do you think a national park *is*, Angie? It is, among other things, a wildlife refuge. There's no difference between this park and a tropical jungle except for temperature and humidity."

"But they let *people* in here. They're not, like, going to let people into a place with dangerous animals lurking about."

"Uh, yes they are. You walk in at your own risk. Read the literature."

We continue discussing wild animals and the curious naïveté of tourists right up until the moment our waiter brings dinner. I think by this time I have Angie reasonably convinced that Yosemite is no children's zoo, and that it's indeed possible to make a wrong turn at the wrong moment and end up face to face with a carnivore who cares nothing for table manners or house guests except how quickly it can dispense with the one and dispose of the other. I also know, however, that Angie will read only what she has to read, that knowledge for its own sake (or even for the sake of her survival) has no place in her purse, and that she thinks truly wild animals are something you find only in *National Geographic* or on the Discovery Channel.

The waiter offers fresh pepper. Angie eyes the mill suspiciously, then nods. The wine steward does his bit and wishes us *bon appétit*.

Angie examines her calf's cheeks carefully—perhaps in an effort to determine which end of the beast they might've come from. I, myself, can't see the difference; it's all just meat. She takes a prudent bite, and the set of her own pert cheeks suggests satisfaction.

We continue our small talk over dinner, but I gain no further knowledge of Angie's character, likes, dislikes or desires—hence, find no way to insinuate myself. At one point, however, I sense that her attention has been arrested by someone or something when she stares out just over my shoulder, blushes, and lowers her eyes to her plate. They remain there for a couple of moments, then rise slowly and cautiously until they reach the level and angle they'd struck earlier—at which point, they blink into a frantic search for something somewhere off in the distance. In spite of my best efforts to keep her engaged in conversation for the remainder of the meal, she's obviously distracted.

Then, out of the blue, "I want to make something of myself, Bruce. I want my life to mean something."

I put down my fork and reach out a compassionate hand, which Angie ignores. "That's what we all want, Angie. But sometimes, just staying alive is as much as we can hope to accomplish in life. Yes, I know, that's not exactly an observation that would turn heads or ears. But it's true—and like so much else in this world—obvious, trite and boring. Life's not a bowl of cherries, ya know. More often than not, it's just a bowl—round, empty and waiting to be filled with whatever falls our way. What you don't want is for someone to suddenly overturn that bo—."

"I don't know anything about bowls or cherries, Bruce. I don't give a turkey's hoot about either. What have I got? This face. *That's* my cherries. That"—a dramatic hand gesture accompanies her words—"and the bit that came with it."

"It's a fine face, Angie. And an excellent bit. You're on your way to fame and glory, no doubt. All you need is a break—and maybe some support in the meantime."

"Yeah, well, support would be nice. Problem is, I ain't got any."

"What? Nobody back home in Iowa?"

"Nobody."

"No parents, no siblings, no foster parents?"

"Nobody."

My hand still hangs in the air, waiting to sweep compassion into her lap if only she'd drop the defense of her dining utensils. Angie gives it an unfriendly eye. "You know, Angie, we could update," I say matter-of-factly.

"Update *what*, Bruce?"

"No. Update. Just update."

"I don't understand."

"It's a *nouvelle* expression. When one partner in a relationship is not at quite the same level of income as the other, but they—ya know—have something working, there's a kind of *quid pro quo*."

"What's the *quid*, Bruce. What's the *quo*?"

"You're getting the hang of this, Angie," I say with a smile. "I'm impressed."

"The *quid*, Bruce. The *quo*. What are they?"

"An exchange."

"What am *I* getting?"

"Financial support."

"What am I *giving*?"

"Think of it as a donation, Angie. No obligation. You give what you can afford to give. What you feel *good* about giving."

"I never feel good about giving."

"But you do like getting, right?"

"Getting's not giving."

"Good point."

"What do I have to *give*, Bruce?"

Our waiter, as if on cue, steps up to the table. "May I take your dishes?"

"Yes, please do," I reply. "At the same time, maybe you could tell us about dessert."

"Well, we have a rather broad selection—all baked on the premises. Shall I run through the list?"

"Please," I say, happy for the interruption.

He begins, only to have Angie stand up and leave when he's barely getting started. He graciously chooses to ignore the affront.

Instead of a sweet, I order coffee and cognac—and tell him I'll check with my dinner partner once she returns from the Ladies' Room. He excuses himself and disappears on his errand. The busboy continues clearing our dishes. When our waiter returns several minutes later with my order, Angie is still not around. In fact, she's gone a good twenty minutes, and it's all I can do not to show a bit of pique when she finally returns, quite flushed.

"I didn't know whether you wanted something," I say. "You didn't seem interested in desser—."

"I wasn't. But I am now." She doesn't even wait for me to call the waiter, but signals him over herself. "I'd like some chocolate mousse and a glass of champagne."

"Certainly, madam."

Her order given, she turns to me. "Bruce, do you have any idea what it means to be a woman? How *difficult* it is?" I stare, nonplussed. "Imagine you're in a teepee, bearing a child... No, rather imagine your village has already been burned down. Your tribe is on the run. You're somewhere between camps, and you feel as if you had to poop a watermelon."

I suddenly need to scratch my eyebrow.

"Nobody cares. Nobody says 'Stop the caravan!' And because you're a woman, you don't dare. You keep moving—just like the rest. This little turd doesn't know, doesn't care about the difference. He's movin' too. He's moving straight down between your legs and looking for an exit. Imagine that, Bruce, and then imagine everyone around you screaming 'We're under attack!' Imagine you're about to drop a baby, and the whole world around you wants to run."

"I'm trying to understand, Angie, but the image of you in a wigwam? I dunno."

"You don't understand, do you, Bruce."

"I *do!*"

"You do."

"Yes. I can imagine."

"You can."

"Yes."

"What *exactly* can you imagine, Bruce?"

"Well... I can imagine the difficulty. Everything around you is chaos, your teepee's going up in smoke, and you're trying to stay centered. The world's going to hell in a hand basket, and you've got this little thing down there wants out—"

"*Big* thing."

"Okay, *big* thing. Doesn't realize the timing's all wrong—the worst possible moment in fact."

"Yeah? And what about *her?*"

"She's fighting just to stay alive—which is my whole point. Sometimes, all of life just boils down to staying alive. Getting up in the morning, going to work, paying the mortgage, raising the children—"

"Who said anything about children?"

"I thought *you* just did. Wasn't that the whole point of your diatribe?—no pun intended, by the way."

"No! My whole point was that I want to succeed, not just survive!"

"Angie, you're sounding like an ad for CitiCorp."

"Whatever."

"'Whatever' is not a watchword for success, Angie."

"What ever it takes, then."

"What if it takes a mate?"

"Huh?"

"What if it takes a mate to survive?"

"Go on."

"I'm offering you an opportunity, Angie."

"Oh, like, a 'once in a lifetime' thingie?"

"Call it what you will. Not everyone gets one."

"What's it gonna cost me?"

"*Cost* you?"

"There's no such thing as a free lunch, Brucie. Especially not with people like you."

"Okay, well, a little nice-nice for starters."

"And for finishers?"

"Well, we'll just have to see," I say as I cross my arms over my chest.

"No, we won't, Bruce. We won't have to see any such thing."

"And why not?"

"Because nice girls finish last. I know. I didn't blow into New York on a whirlwind of blind trust. The hayseeds lifted from my eyes long before I boarded the bus."

"Your metaphor, Angie, is mixed. I'm afraid I'm clueless as to what you're leading up to."

"I'm not leading *up* to anything, Brucie. I'm leading *out!*"—and with that, Angie takes the last of her champagne in one gulp, throws her napkin down and stands up from the table. "Thank you for a *lovely* dinner. When you eat here tomorrow evening—alone, I dare say—may I suggest the calf's cheeks? They would, if you don't mind another mixed metaphor, seem to be just your cup of tea."

She walks away without another word, and I pick up my snifter. I detest scenes in public places and now wonder whether ours has drawn any attention. Once again, and as if on cue, our waiter approaches. I ask for another cognac and the check; he obliges with a nod as if absolutely nothing had happened. I decide to express my gratitude in the tip.

When he brings me the check and the second cognac, I tell him I'd prefer to take both in The Great Lounge—and ask that he kindly find me a comfortable chair next to the fireplace. He nods again and disappears. When he returns moments later, it's merely to suggest, with the gesture of an outstretched arm, that I follow him to the newer berth he's chosen for my comfortable repose. I follow him out of the dining room as if he's a tug and I'm his luxury liner in tow—the cognac and check our only reason for being tied to one another, but a good and sufficient reason nonetheless, as the waters in this otherwise safe harbor have turned decidedly choppy.

The word "manservant" suddenly comes to mind, and for the first time in my life I understand what it means to have one—how pleasing, how conducive to composure and a sense of well-being. I dig down into my pocket and withdraw my room key. He bends down slightly to note the room number, then heads off to settle my account. I sit back into my chair to contemplate the fire. I know I've got a couple of twenties in my pocket, and I suspect the sight of double-digit denominations will please him no end.

He returns moments later and hands me the check once again, now resting in leather. I sign it with gusto, then retrieve the twenties in the cup of my hand, which I extend for a man-to-manservant shake, letting the cash speak its *lingua franca* for both of us.

"Everything satisfactory, sir?"

"Couldn't have been better," I say. "You run a fine establishment here." "Run" as the presiding action verb on his résumé is something he clearly savors, may never have heard in connection with his own name, may only dream about.

"Thank you. If I can be of any further service, please don't hesitate."

"Actually, there is something—," I venture. "It would require keen powers of observation and the utmost discretion." I eye him conspiratorially, and he lunges at the bait.

"I'm your man for both, sir."

"Well, it's like this, really—," I begin slowly, wanting to lure him in of course, but also not wanting to seem too obvious, too eager for his help.

He glances back once over both shoulders to make sure no one else might be eavesdropping.

"I'm here as a kind of chaperone to a colleague's daughter. My mission is to bring her to an appreciation of one of Mother Nature's wonders—Yosemite, of course—but to make certain, at the same time, she doesn't get sidetracked by any of Mother Nature's *other* wonders—if you get my drift."

"I do, sir. I once had a young daughter of my own, and I indelibly understand."

"Hmm. Quite. I don't want to mother-hen the poor girl to death, you understand, but I have a responsibility."

"Yes, sir. I'm with you on that. Why, just this evening, sir, inasmuch as I'm enumerating our dessert selection for your deliberation, she practically leaps out of her chair. You maybe didn't realize—" I try to conceal a keen interest in what he has to say, but I feel my throat constrict and my face redden as he continues. "—how she seemed to be in such a rush to get somewhere."

"The ladies' room, I believe—."

"Well, yes and no, sir. She certainly headed off in that direction, I grant you. But a young man she's been trading glances with much of the evening jumps up just as sudden and follows her out of the dining room. When I walk past the restrooms on my way to the coffee station, there she is, plain as daylight, waiting for him. He flies to her, she runs to him, and they both walk out the back door arm in arm."

"Well, there you are," I say, affecting a quiet air of complacency. "That's just the kind of thing I'm here to circumvent."

"You and me both, sir—if I may be so bold."

"You may indeed, uh—."

"'Name's Arthur, sir, if that's what you'd now be asking. Glad to be of service."

"Arthur? Seymour here. Bruce Seymour. Please just call me 'Bruce'."

"Yes, sir, Mr. Seymour," he says as he extends a solid manservant's hand and I reach up to shake it.

"In the meantime, Arthur, I shouldn't want you to lack reward for your efforts," I say as I dig my free hand down into my pocket for another twenty.

"Reward won't be necessary, Mr. Seymour. Like I said, I, too, have a daughter. Let's just consider this a man-to-man favor."

"Man to man, Arthur," I say barely above a whisper, "I suspect I'm in very capable hands here. That we're *all* in capable hands here. And that one other young man in particular had better mind his Ps and Qs where my Ang—, my colleague's daughter, is concerned."

"They don't call me 'the watchman' here at the Ahwahnee for nothing, Mr. Seymour. I believe I've earned my stripes over the years."

"No doubt you have, Arthur. No doubt you have." I take a last, long sip from my snifter and hold the glass up in silent salute. Arthur takes it from my hand and withdraws with a bow. "Until tomorrow night then, Arthur."

"Until then, sir."

Chapter FOUR

I go immediately to our room in the expectation that a contrite Angie, finally reconciled to her ungratefulness, will be awaiting my arrival — hat in hand, as it were. I have every intention of extracting whatever price she's willing to pay, penitence being as much at the pleasure of the aggrieved as it is at the pain of the transgressor. I have no idea who this young man might be; still less, any concern about his welfare; least of all, a thought about his retribution or damnation. The only compensation I wish to gain for this whole sordid business is Angie's complete submission — that she should *beg* me to deliver her from her misguided need to look anywhere but to me for guidance, inspiration, and yes — transcendence. I and I alone will be her redeemer, I'm thinking as I open the door —.

There's no one in the room. "Angie," I call, half-expecting to hear a tearful "Yes, Bruce?" from somewhere within, but I hear only the sound of my own voice.

The thing now is to remain calm, think clearly, act decisively, I think to myself as I get undressed and pull back the bed sheets — but not before setting up my alarm clock with its luminous numbers and hands facing my pillow.

I'm solidly asleep long before both hands on my alarm clock reach twelve, and I have no idea how much time has passed when I first hear sounds outside our room, catch a glimmer of light from the hallway as she slips in through the door, then listen to her labored breathing as she waits for her eyes to adjust to the darkness. I half-open one of my own and note the hour: 3:00 a.m.

When I awake shortly after eight the next morning, the sun is lurking through the curtains. At the moment I realize where I now am, I hear the sound of heavy breathing from somewhere down on the floor, then remember I'm not alone in the room. I hoist myself up on an elbow and look in Angie's direction. Through a mass of scattered blond hair, I see the back of flannel pajamas covered with little teddy-bears in various states of dance over the hills and dales of her body. "Lions and tigers and bears—oh, my indeed!" I think to myself.

I get out of bed and take a shower, dry off and walk right out into the room to get a fresh set of clothes. Nothing compels my modesty at this point, and *less* than nothing compels me to consider her need to sleep undisturbed—and so, I make no effort to cloak or muffle any aspect of my presence. I am, in fact, quite disposed to have her wake up and find me exactly as I am.

Strange it is, I think, that she doesn't awaken.

I leave the room and descend to the dining room for breakfast, where I'm met almost immediately by Arthur wearing a grave expression. "Breakfast for one, Mr. Seymour?" he asks, but it's clear he already knows the answer.

"Yes, Arthur, breakfast for one. The young lady will be sleeping in this morning."

He grabs a menu and escorts me to our table of the previous evening, then goes without a word to fetch orange juice and coffee. When he returns an instant later, I hand him back the menu.

"A couple of eggs over easy, please, Arthur. And a double portion of bacon. I've got an expedition of sorts planned for today, and I can use the extra protein."

"An exhibition, sir? I should've thought last night's exhibition was more than sufficient."

I find his choice of words distinctly unsettling—and not just the malapropism—but I realize the tone is not directed at me or at anything *I* might've said or done. "Yes?" I ask, giving him plenty of latitude to unburden himself of the news he's so clearly eager to share.

His eyes dart first one way, then the other before he bends over almost within whispering distance of my ear. "Well, sir, as you might guess—out here in the middle of nowhere—most of the help at the Ahwahnee live on the premises, just beyond the guest cottages—."

"Guest cottages?"

"Indeed, sir. They're usually empty this time of year. But in late spring, summer and fall, they're every bit as busy as the main building."

"I see —."

"In any case, I finish up here in the restaurant not much more than an hour after you, yourself, have retired for the night. I'm making my way to the dormitory, minding my own business, when I hear sounds from one of the cottages and notice that a window has been forced. I'm not a Peeping Tom, mind you, and so I don't approach to get me a better look. Instead, I just slow down a bit — well, stand still, really — to 'ave a look at the moon. I don't know whether you noticed last night, but it was a fu —."

"Yes, and — ?" I say. I notice — and then Arthur notices — that I'm now pressing the tines of my fork down into the table cloth. "Please go on," I say as I make a concerted effort to modulate my voice and lay my fork back down in its uneventful place.

"Well, sir, like I say, those sounds. Didn't seem natural. Sounded like animal noises. I thought it might be animals — we have plenty of wild ones out here, you know."

"Yes, I know."

"A body's got to be careful —."

"Please get on with it, Arthur."

My inadvertent command causes him to stand upright, almost to attention. "There's really nothing more to say, Mr. Seymour. I went on to the dormitory, went to bed, went to sleep. Some time around three o'clock, I think it was, I hear a door shut — or what sounds like a door shutting. I don't pay it any mind. Instead, I go back to sleep."

"That's it?"

"That's it — except for this morning."

"This morning? What did you see this morning?"

"I'm coming over for the breakfast shift. It's still quite early, the sun's barely up, and I see this boy — the same one I saw last night with your young lady — in jogging shorts and sneakers."

"Yes, the same boy —."

"He's putting the window aright."

"He's putting the window aright?"

"Yes, that he is. I stop a while, quite out of sight — and when he's finished, he looks around the entrance to the cottage. He then brushes his sneaker across the snow where, I suppose, footprints had been left."

"Footprints had been left?"

"Yes, well, sir, I don't want to say — you know, category-wise — that

I know who left 'em."

"No, Arthur, of course you don't. We can, however, make certain assumptions."

"Yes, sir. Assumptions are what we can make. If you'll now allow me, sir —" he says with what I take to be a clear signal of his desire to leave me to my musings and go about his usual business.

"Of course, Arthur. And please make sure the bacon is crisp."

"Crisp, sir."

When he brings my breakfast several minutes later, neither of us is disposed to continue our earlier conversation. I eat quickly and in silence, eager to get on with the original purpose of my visit to Yosemite. In twenty minutes, I'm done and pushing back my chair at the same time I signal Arthur for the check. I sign it and slip him a five-dollar bill, which he acknowledges with a nod.

"I don't know that we'll be lunching here today, Arthur, but we'll certainly see you this evening for dinner."

"Very good, sir. I wish you happy hunting and a most pleasant sojourn, wherever one or the other might take you today."

"A pleasant sojourn is what I intend, Arthur," I say with a smile. The word itself seems to fit the room's décor.

The first thing I hear a few minutes later as I slip my key into the door of our room is the sound of the shower. I decide to sit and wait to hear what Angie has to say about the previous evening — about her abrupt departure from the dining room; about where she might've spent the hours between midnight and three o'clock in the morning. Perhaps she'll have nothing to say at all. Perhaps, instead, this shower is a kind of ablution — her preparation for self-sacrifice upon the high altar of my forgiveness. I admit I have a certain soft spot for penitence — and I'm eager to hear her full confession.

I don't have long to wait. She exits the bathroom, fully dressed, in a flurry, and drying her hair with a bath towel. I wonder where she gets the energy after so little sleep. No matter. I have in mind to put that youthful energy to good use.

"Sleep well?" I ask.

"Very well, thank you."

"What shall we do today, Angie? Take a hike? Take a drive? Explore the park?" I'm secretly hoping she'll suggest, by word or gesture, that we simply sleep in.

"If it's okay by you, Bruce, I think I'll just hang around the hotel.

You run along and do whatever it is you want to do."

I make a supreme effort to restrain my anger. This is *not* what I'd intended for the price of a cross-country flight and two nights' stay in a very expensive—dare I say *romantic* —setting. "Angie, we're here for a purpose. Time is now of the essence. We'll be checking out early tomorrow morning and heading back to San Francisco. I told you I had business to conduct—."

"Yes, I know, Bruce. I'm well aware we've scheduled a shoot. But I thought we were in agreement on a sunset shoot. Sunset's still several hours away."

"Yes it is, Angie. But a little quality time together might make this seem like less of a chore, more of a holiday. You can't do much shopping out here in the woods," I say with what I know is a bit of fashionable snarkiness.

"Shopping is not what I had in mind, Bruce."

"Then what *did* you have in mind, Angie?"

She leaves off towel-drying her hair and looks up to face me directly. "Carousing. I thought I'd spend the day carousing," she says trading snarky tit for tat.

"Fine," I say as I practically jump out of my chair. "Go and carouse. Just be back here at four and in your body stocking. We've got only one chance to do this, and today's the day. If you're not here at four—ready, willing and waiting—you can find your own way back to San Francisco and New York. And then you can find yourself a new agent."

"I'll be here at four."

I pick up the car keys from the on-duty valet on the way out of the hotel, then locate our car parked between two large mounds of snow, both melting down like a bit of day-old news. From the temperature and a quick look at the bits of sky I can see peeking through the Redwood branches overhead, a fresh snowfall would have to be far down on my list of predictions for the next twenty-four hours. However, I haven't checked the forecast; I know that storms can spin up out of nowhere and spill suddenly in a microclimate like this one; and I have to admit that my predictions of late haven't exactly been of the crystal ball variety.

I jump in, start the engine, ease out of the lot. I've got a map of the park—but am really in no mood to see the sites. Instead, I spend the next several hours driving in circles, killing time, watching the hands move around my watch towards four, and thinking.

When I return to the hotel just before the appointed hour, there's still

114

plenty of light—though it's an afternoon light, moving inexorably towards dusk. The temperature has also dropped by several degrees, and I make a mental note to check at the front desk for an update on the weather.

As I enter the front door and make my way to reception, I glance in the direction of The Great Lounge. There, seated in front of the fireplace and looking from a distance like two happy mourning doves cooing and pecking and completely oblivious of their surroundings, are Angie and her young man. A quantity of bile rises in my throat as I quickly turn my attention to Meredith at the front desk.

"Mr. Seymour, good afternoon."

"And the same to you, Meredith," I manage to squeeze out with a quick smile. "What's the forecast for this evening?"

Meredith's eyebrows knit together into one long line of consternation. "I'm afraid there's a storm on the way. We could have a foot of snow by morning. They're good about the roads up here, so no need to worry about travel tomorrow. But you may want to stay close to camp this evening." And then, just as if she has suddenly remembered some instruction from basic training, she lights up, all smiles. "We've got plenty of wood for the fire, and the chef has added a few new specials to this evening's dinner menu. You and Mrs. Seymour won't want for the comforts of home, Mr. Seymour."

"Thank you, Meredith. I'm certain that with you at the helm, we won't. Not for a single one." I make a mental note to write a letter of commendation to her boss as I pick up a book of matches with the hotel's name and address embossed on the rear panel.

I turn around and head off towards the elevator, but not without first glancing again in the direction of The Great Lounge. The loveseat in front of the fireplace is empty.

When I arrive at the elevator, I note that it is, at that very instant, stopping at the third floor—time enough, if she hurries, for Angie to get back to our room and change into something more appropriate to *outdoor* recreation before I arrive at the same destination. Up till now, I might've hoped to catch her in mid-change. Now, however, I want no surprises to interfere with, or otherwise alter, my plan. I tear all but three of the matches out of the book, drop them into a dustbin next to the elevator, and put the book back into my pocket.

Sure enough, in the time it takes for the elevator to descend to lobby level, pick me and a few other passengers up and deposit us at the second and third floors, I find that Angie has changed into her bodysuit and thrown on a loose-fitting sweater that reaches to mid-thigh. Flushed, freshly made up, and with a happy face she can have acquired only after years of practice and polish, she greets me like a dear friend.

"Bruce!"

"You're ready?" I ask.

"I am. Couldn't be ever readier even if I were the bunny!"

"Hmm."

"Brucie, why so glum?"

"Not glum, Angie. Just concentrating on this afternoon's plan."

"Well, then, let's execute!"

"I think you might want to put on a few more clothes. It could get cold out there," I add, knowing that she will do exactly the contrary of what I suggest.

"Nonsense! It feels like spring!" she says. And suspecting that she's spent the entire day indoors and at least part of it in front of the fire, I'm sure it does. As she stands up and moves past me towards the door, I catch a whiff of her—an almost overwhelming combination of natural musk and "Come Hither"—her perfume, of course, of choice.

"Angie, you might want to lose the perfume. Sweet smells attract bears, and we don't want to meet any of them on this trail. They'll be coming out of hibernation—hungry and reckless."

"Brucie, don't be ridiculous! There are no bears in this park. At least not *dangerous* ones!"

"I know only what I read, Angie." And with that, I grab a flashlight and my camera, tear off a couple of heads from the dozen roses still standing in a vase next to the bed, and follow her out the door. While we wait for the elevator to arrive, Angie asks—as if she might actually have any real interest in our little project now that it's all about her—how long the trek out to Mirror Lake will take. I tell her an hour—plus or minus. A raised eyebrow tells me she suspects it's more of "plus" than of "minus." I let the suspicion ride.

An hour and several of Angie's exasperated sighs later, I once again see the sign indicating that Mirror Lake is still seven tenths of a mile off. I know from my previous excursion out to the lake that just beyond this point is a wide service road running directly back to the hotel, and I'm now careful to steer Angie away from it and onto a narrow path leading through the woods. It's from here on that I begin to drop rose petals at regular intervals.

Angie stops and turns around at one point just as I drop a petal. "What on *earth*?" she says as she puts her hands on her hips.

"Just a precaution," I say. "I want to make sure we find our way back to the .7-mile marker." At the same time, I realize her pose is a great "woman in her natural element" kind of thing. "Hold it now," I say as I remove the cover from my lens, then focus and snap.

Angie guffaws. "What are we, Hansel and Gretel? You are *too* much, Brucie!"

"One can never be too careful, Angie." I take a second insurance shot.

"Indeed —!" This single word is as much energy as she's willing to spend on my apparent folly, and I notice she's somewhat winded from the walk. At the same time, it's growing chilly even if the sky is only partially overcast, and I wonder whether she now regrets she didn't take my earlier advice to dress in a way more appropriate to the setting than to her mood. In fact, when we finally arrive at our destination, a few flakes are beginning to fall, and Angie shivers as she squints and looks up at the sky.

"It's just a single raincloud. It'll pass soon enough," I say to reassure her — and the snow does indeed stop almost as quickly as it had started.

I point out the rock to her — just a small leap from where she's now standing. She looks at it as if calculating in her mind whether she can bridge the gap without falling backwards or overshooting and falling headfirst into the water. I assure her she can do it, then remind her of our purpose — her book — and ask her to lose the sweater. She jumps, settles down onto the rock, then eyes me skeptically as she removes her sweater and hands it back to me over our watery divide.

I tie both arms of her sweater around my waist — a warm embrace at last! I think.

While I pretend to be working out angles and backdrops, Angie is perched on the rock — very Little Mermaid-like — and shivering. I take my time. Her occasional shivers turn into a regular tremble. I take more time. I note she's losing all hint of pink in her face. I conjure up new angles; the mountains behind us remain stubbornly as they have for millennia, though their color and hue are turning slowly to monochrome in the fading sunlight.

"Bruce, can't we get started? *Please.*"

"Problem is the light, Angie. We've lost most of the natural light I wanted for these shots. I really hate to have to use a flash. If only we'd started out sooner —." I say this last in the expectation that she'll recognize and acknowledge the fault for where it lies.

"I understand," she says as she drops her head to her chest — as much in contrition, I assume, as in an effort to expose less of her neck to

117

the cold.

"Hey, *I've* got an idea. Why don't we build a fire?" I dig down into my pants pocket and withdraw the book of only three matches. "We've got the spark—" I say as I hold up the book, then lay it down a leap away "—now, all we need is some fuel. You and a campfire with this backdrop? Marvelous!" Angie nods slowly in resignation as she registers my placement of the book of matches. "Let me go fetch some wood," I say as I move off into the woods.

Over the course of the next half hour, I'm a diligent wood-gatherer. I'm careful in each instance to head out in a different direction, return by a different route, carry only a log or two each time. I never bring back kindling, but Angie's too self-absorbed or perhaps too cold to notice my omission. I offer comforting words upon each return, tell her it will only be a matter of a few minutes more before we have a blazing fire—just like the one in The Great Lounge. I suspect this reminder gives her some additional warmth—however much warmth a fond memory can give as the thermometer inches inexorably south.

Almost no light remains in the sky, the temperature is certainly below freezing, and the snow has begun to fall once again when I grab the flashlight and prepare to head out one last time. "B-b-b-ruce, can't we p-p-p-lease start the fire?" Angie asks pathetically through trembling lips.

"Of *course* we can, Angie. Brucie now just has to fetch some kindling. Very difficult, you know, to start a fire without kindling," I say in the most pedantic tone I can muster. "Unfortunately, I haven't been able to find any so far," I lie. "I'll have to go further back into the woods. This may take a while. Just try to stay warm—think warm thoughts."

She nods slowly, dejectedly, and I set out via a circuitous route to find the path that had led us to this spot in the first place. I see the last of the rose petals I'd dropped to mark that path, pick it up and thrust it deep into my pocket. I continue along the same path, bending down occasionally to retrieve rose petals as I walk, right up until my flashlight finds the .7-mile marker. From this point on, I know I won't find any more petals, but they're no longer necessary for me to navigate my return to the hotel. I've made this trek twice. And although I suspect I could find my way back under a full moon, the snow—now falling in ever-thickening sheets—tells me there will be no moon tonight, full or otherwise. Instead, I depend upon my flashlight right up until the point at which the hotel's own exterior lights illuminate my path.

Chapter FIVE

Three hours later, a fine dinner tumbling in my belly while a cognac and coffee wait within easy reach, I sit in perfect contentment on a loveseat in front of a blazing fire in a cavernous room of a fine hotel. This loveseat — like its twin just opposite me — is set at a ninety-degree angle to the fire, and I turn my head to look across the room and out the floor-to-ceiling windows at curtain call upon curtain call of large, billowy snowflakes — and then re-focus on the pitch black emptiness just out of range of the hotel's lights. The flames of the fire in front of me, I note with some relish, reflect ghoulishly off the windowpanes — orange specters dancing for my perusal and with no other care in the world but that I should be entertained.

"Excuse me, sir — ." The sound of a human voice abruptly interrupts my reverie. I look to its source and see, standing off to the side of my loveseat, the young man I believe might have been Angie's...Angie's what? I'm still not really sure.

"Yes?"

"I was looking for your daughter. She didn't dine with you this evening." He has, I must admit, a certain air of refinement. What a pity, I think.

"My daughter?"

"Yes, your daughter."

"I don't have a daughter."

"Angelina."

"Who?"

"Angelina. Your daughter. The girl you were dining with yesterday evening."

"No, no. There must be some mistake. And you, by the way, would be—?"

"No, I saw you!" A whine has crept into his voice, and I don't like it. It reminds me of Angie's whine. Lucky for both of us, he recovers quickly. "Sorry. The name's 'Crandall'," he says as he extends a young gentleman's hand.

I ignore the hand. "What you saw, Crandall, is me with a dinner companion. If you must know—and I don't exactly know why you must—with my employee, Roweena."

He appears not to hear—or *want* to hear—the correction. "Is she not feeling well? Is she not coming down to dinner this evening?"

"Unfortunately, she's had to return to San Francisco—well, to Oakland really."

"To *San Francisco?*" He's whining again.

"Yes."

"But I thought she was from New York. That she's a model in New York."

"Hah! Either you've got the wrong girl, or that employee of mine has *some* imagination!"

"And her name's Rowee—?"

"Roweena. She works for me. In Oakland. She manages one of my stores."

"She *manages a store?* What kind of store—?" he asks, mouth agape.

"Well, if you must know, I own a chain of pet stores. Roweena is a manager-in-training at one of them."

"A *pet* store?" Gullibility in another lends such a feast. In spite of the three-course dinner I've just enjoyed, I feel suddenly ravenous for more.

"Yes, a pet store. She's a real hit with the animals. They just *eat* her up," I say with a chuckle.

"She won't be coming back tonight or tomorrow?" he asks, wearing disappointment like a Purple Heart.

"I'm afraid not. She's filling in on an emergency basis. Animals have to be fed, you know. Why, —I glance at my watch—I suspect she's feeding them even as we speak."

"I see."

"Yes, well, duty calls — and so do animals when they're hungry. Lucky for me, I have an employee as conscientious as Roweena to attend to them. No muss, no fuss — just back to work."

"I see — ," he says one last time, though more to himself than to me as he turns slowly around and walks off.

"Toodaloo, Crandall," I say under my breath before returning my attention to the fire and to my musing. The flames are licking the top of the fireplace and sending showers of sparks up the chimney. The heat is so intense, I involuntarily retreat back into the loveseat; feel the warmth invading and settling into its fabric; finally get up and wander over to one of the rear windows in search of cool relief.

I look out into snowfall and the impenetrable darkness just beyond and remember something I'd once read in some obscure monograph on death and dying. Of the means by which you could attain that unfavorable but inevitable end — I'm paraphrasing — "alone" and "in agony" were the least desirable. Agony could take many forms, of course, but specific mention of your still living, breathing, *gasping* flesh in the teeth and claws of a large animal just fresh out of hibernation was not one of them. Perhaps the author was squeamish. Perhaps he had no experience with wild animals. Perhaps he'd never read about *accidents* in a wildlife refuge like this one.

Bears could be particularly nasty when famished. In no mood for nuts or berries after six months in a cave, they'd simply lift their nostrils to the air and follow the scent to its source, then rip into the prize without so much as a how-do-you-do if it offered no resistance. (A girl succumbing to hypothermia, I surmise, would offer barely an iota.) The softer bits would go first, of course — the places you, yourself, might recognize as ticklish or particularly sensitive to heat and cold: armpits; the groin; cheeks of either variety. The bear might or might not first administer a *coup de grâce*. If so, and if the force of its paw didn't immediately break your neck, the claw would most assuredly tear off half your face in its swipe.

A mountain lion, on the other hand, would go straight for the throat and might first strangle you before tearing out your trachea and esophagus, severing your head, and settling down to devour the remainder of your still-warm carcass. Big cats were merciful in that way. Too bad there were considerably fewer lions — never mind tigers — than bears in Yosemite.

And while you wait, cold well beyond numb in the pitch black, having expended three matches in a futile effort to ignite a hard log, now watching the last of your hopes snuff out with the last of the three matches? Hardly refreshing. There's no one to call out to as your predator finds you quite easily by his nose alone—though you can always try calling out to mommy. Mortally wounded soldiers and men with a noose sitting snug around their necks frequently—though not with any notable success—do.

I return to the loveseat; finish the last of my coffee and cognac; place cup and snifter carefully back down on the table. I then walk casually up to the front desk. Meredith, seemingly always present, ever-watchful, ever-courteous, greets me. I return her greeting, inform her that we will be departing early in the morning, report that our stay has been nothing less than magical, ask that she have the final bill delivered to my room during the night. She answers each bit of news or request with a cordial nod.

"By the way, Meredith," I ask just before leaving the front desk. "The Crandall party? Do you recognize the name? We had the pleasure of making their acquaintance yesterday evening. I neglected to ask for a card."

"Oh, yes, of course—the Crandalls," Meredith says as she flips through her index of guest names. "Of Grosse Pointe. They're regulars this time of year. Delightful family. Let me see—," her voice trails off as she locates what she's looking for, writes down the name and address on a piece of hotel stationery, then puts it into an envelope, which she hands over to me with her ever-courteous smile.

"Thank you so much, Meredith. I'll certainly treat this with the utmost discretion. Goodnight."

"Goodnight, Mr. Seymour. And *bon voyage* back to New York. Do please come and see us again soon."

"Most assuredly, Meredith."

A new "American Tragedy," I muse as I drift off to sleep. Funny, I haven't given a thought to Dreiser since my Groton days.

I sleep exceedingly well.

Just after dawn the next morning, I slip out of the hotel with all of our belongings and take them to the car. At least a foot of snow has fallen overnight, but the parking lot and roads into and out of the Ahwahnee compound have already been plowed. I drive out with ease and enter the long service road leading me to Highway 120—and ultimately, to San Francisco.

On one stretch of road called Big Oak, and just before exiting Yosemite, traffic—as light as it is at this hour of the morning—is being detoured, and I learn the reason for it minutes later: a combination of avalanche and rockslide has buried the road. I wonder how long it will take the authorities to determine whether there might be a car or two buried beneath — and, if so, whether bears and mountain lions will get there first. Rescue people in a place like this are the best at what they do, I figure. But then, nature — after a long sleep and in the roar of hunger — is bigger, badder, even better.

On a two-lane road leading to the airport in San Francisco, I look for a Dempsey Dumpster, but then spot a thrift shop, pull over, and take out Angie's things. It would, I think, be a waste just to dump them. The lady who takes my donation doesn't ask; I don't tell.

A few doors down, I find a shop selling cell phones and buy a disposable unit.

I continue the last few miles to the airport; check in the rental car, then myself and my baggage; make my way to the gate. As I'm passing through the people-feeder tube to the plane two hours later, I suddenly realize: as special as our something might've been, I didn't lose my heart in San Francisco. Hmm, I think.

Chapter SIX

Back in New York, and after having alighted from the Lexington Line at the 34th Street stop on my brisk way to Monday morning work, I stop in at a newsstand and buy a copy each of *The National Inquirer, Star* and *The Globe*. I figure if there's a story—and if anyone's going to cover it—one of these three mavericks will. Grist for the tabloid mill originating anywhere west of the Hudson is not going to find its way into *The Post* or *The Daily News*—unless and until, that is, someone discovers that the grist belongs to one of our own. Then, of course, she's suddenly one of *ours*—so it's big news. But I know it's my duty to Angie to make sure that never happens. It would be a hell-of-a career boost, no doubt, but Angie can't really use that kind of boost just now. I suspect, even before opening any of the three papers I now carry folded under my arm, that her rather short-lived career is all played out.

Imagine my surprise, then, when I get to the office, close and lock the door, and spread the three papers out. I obviously had it wrong weeks ago when I suggested that Angie wasn't a cover kinda girl. Right there on the front page of each is the identical forensic photo: a headless and limbless stump of a thing, totally unidentifiable as human or even animal were it not for the three papers' respective headlines: "Tragedy in America's Playground"; "Bear-hugged to Death!"; and, in what even *I* have to say is a rather tasteless single-word summation of the unfortunate event, "Dogmeat."

The short text alongside each facsimile of the same photograph tells the "what," "where" and "how" of the circumstances of the death and dismemberment of an anonymous and unidentifiable young lady. The "why" and "who," unanswered, stand out like teasers—in bold, in fact, for the hard-of-reading or slow-to-get-it. I flip through the "Dogmeat" paper for a location and a telephone number. *Some*body, *some*where actually has to write this stuff, and I wanna find him.

Unsuccessful in finding anything in the paper that might lead me to its source, I turn to Google—and bingo! Practically everything I need—including a reprint of the photo in living color—on my screen and at my fingertips. I dig the disposable cell phone out of my coat pocket and dial the 800 number—and a not-particularly-friendly voice answers. Where do they find these people? I wonder.

"I'm calling about the page one article, 'Dogmeat,' in today's edition," I announce. Silence. "Hello?"

"What about it?"

"I'd like to speak with whoever covered the story."

"Who are you?"

"That doesn't really matter. I have something that may be of interest to him or her."

"To her."

"I figured as much.

"How'd you *figure* as much?"

"It's a human interest story. It's all about animals."

"What'd you wanna talk to her for? You an animal lover?"

"As I said, I believe I may have something of interest."

"Of what possible interest?"

"For her to decide. Can you please patch me through?"

"Hold on, animal lover."

The phone goes dead for several seconds. I don't realize the connection is broken until I get extraterrestrial sounds followed by a disembodied voice asking me to hang up and try again. I do.

"I believe we lost our connection," I say when I hear the same unfriendly voice greet me in the same uninviting way.

"Hold on."

"Be happy to. But please don't disconnect us this ti—," I feel compelled to add before the voice of friendship and brotherly love abruptly cuts me off.

A businesslike female voice picks up seconds later. "Yes?"

"You wrote the story 'Dogmeat?'" I ask.

"Yeah, but not the headline. We have specialists for that. What'd ya want? I'm busy."

"I'm sure you are. I'd love to meet them, by the way. I—."

"We never let them out. We keep them in cages."

For someone who's ostensibly "busy," I realize this woman's at least got a sense of humor, and doesn't mind spending some time in exercising it. I figure I might have a good—or at least amusing—negotiating partner.

"As it happens, I know the identity of the body in question. Your article suggests you don't—and that you're a little short on clues."

"Friend of yours? Your neighbor's kid? Your own kid? Nah, you wouldn't be calling if it was your own kid."

"They obviously did right when they put you on the case. You think quick."

"Story, not case. I'm a reporter, remember? I'm only interested in selling stories—uh, newspapers—not in solving the world's problems."

"Right." Silence.

"You're calling from a 415 area code. San Francisco, right?"

"Smart reporter. Smart girl, uh, woman."

"Smart Caller I.D. So you think you know who she is. What're you pitching?"

"A photograph—maybe two."

"We already got a photo, or didn't you see the article." It wasn't a question.

"I saw it. What you have is only marginally of interest. I have something better."

"'Marginally,' huh? What're you, a college professor?"

"She was a model. Drop-dead gorgeous. Cover kinda girl." Silence. "*Hallo?*"

"How do you know this?"

"Doesn't matter how I know it. I know it. And I've got photographs to prove it."

"What's your interest?"

"What's *any* of our interest? I got a mortgage to pay." Silence.

"Nah. You could be any jerk just trying to make up a connection to turn a quick buck."

"Maybe. But maybe n—."

"Call me back in five minutes. I've gotta pee."

"What's your name?"

"Lasner. What's yours?"

"Anonymous."

126

"Very funny, anonymous." Click.

I decide to give it ten. If she's going to turn up the heat on me this early in the game, I figure I can return the kindness—let her think about it for a while and get antsy. The story's a one-day thriller if all she's got is the stump. Put Angie's modeling pictures right next to that stump, however, and the paper'll sell out for months as the investigation develops. She knows it. Right about now, she's seeing her own name in lights—or at least on the Editor's list of promotables.

Problem for me, I've got to figure how far out on a limb I'm willing to go—and how much her paper's willing to pay to grease my way out there. So far, she's buying the bit about my San Francisco address. Good thinking on my part to buy that cell phone locally. Now, I've got to figure out how to make the exchange without getting burned. I figure I'll use the leverage I have with her interest in the photos to see what she proposes.

I call back and decide not to engage in any more chit-chat with the receptionist. "Ms. Lasner, please."

Almost instantly, "Mr. Anonymous, of San Francisco?"

"The very one."

"I've talked with my boss. We're not interested."

"Too bad," I say. "I've got studio shots, of course—but also one of her, intact and trail-blazing the day of the, uh, mishap." Silence. I decide not to interrupt it, as I sense she's covering the receiver and discussing the matter with a second party.

"A picture of her in the vicinity of the crime?"

"Who said it was a crime?" I ask.

"She didn't go out there to sunbathe, Mister. It was snowing like nobody's business the day or night she went out. All they found on her— or on what was left of her—were shreds of what appeared to be a body stocking. That, and a sweater she'd apparently taken off earlier in the day. It was buried under a foot of snow."

"I'll leave the investigation and the motive—if there was on—to you."

"Did *you* take the picture?"

"I didn't say that. All I said was I have it."

"Yeah, sure, but you'd have to have been pretty close to the scene of the, uh, 'mishap' to have the picture."

"I didn't say I have the original. I have only a digital copy. It was sent to me this morning."

"By who?"

"By *whom*."

"Okay, Professor. By *whom?*"

"By Anonymous II."

"You're a hilariously anonymous bunch." Pause. "How ya know it's the same girl?"

"She's wearing the sweater you mentioned—over a body stocking."

"So?"

"The *face*, Ms. Lasner. Remember? I have her studio shots. I'm her agent." Silence.

"Call me back," she says. Click.

I'm revealing a lot more than I'd intended, and my pulse proves it. However, I've now got her interest. I give it another five or so while I walk around my office to try to take the edge off.

My cell rings. There's only one other person in the world who knows I've got this phone, and that other person is possibly holding enough payola to reimburse Angie's and my little trip out to California—as well as to meet my mortgage payment. I pull out my wallet and frantically search for the receipt for the purchase of the phone—on the back of which I've taken the precaution of writing down the number. I then take the incoming call before it rings off or goes to voicemail, and I give only the telephone number by way of answer, but no name.

"Roberts here."

"Yes, Mr. Roberts. What can I do for you?"

"You spoke earlier with Ms. Lasner."

"I did. And you are—?"

"Her boss."

"She's a fine reporter. Shortly due for a promotion and a raise, no doubt."

"Cut the shit. You got photos, right?"

"I do."

"And you can make a positive I.D.?"

"I can."

"You got a name?"

"No names—except for Roberts and Lasner. I deal in the world of images, not of names. You deal in the world of print—and occasionally of imag—."

"The girl has family. We'd first have to notify them before we run a thing like this. Out of consideration, you understand."

"Yes, of course. 'Dogmeat.' Out of consideration."

"I don't make up the headlines. We have speci—."

"'Special people.' I know." Silence. I let it sit.

"How much do you want?"

"A hundred."

"A hundred dollars?"

"Very funny."

"I try to be when occasion warrants."

"Okay, Mr. Roberts, let's stay on topic, shall we? I've got a photo of the girl, in Yosemite, taken the day of the event. I've also got enough studio shots to let you run her picture for half a dozen issues. She's a cutie, trust me. You figure out how you can get me a hundred Gs in friendly bills, I get you the photos any way you like 'em."

"*Quid pro quo,* huh?"

I smile. "'Nice to hear a live man speak a dead language. I usually only hear that kind of talk from lawyers and academics."

"We do our best to keep Latin alive around here. Remember, we're a *language resource.*"

"Oh, yeah. I'd almost forgotten. 'Dogmeat.' *De mortuis nil nisi bonum,*" I add for our mutual edification. Silence.

"As a token of good faith, are you willing to send me the picture of her wearing the sweater before you see the money?"

"As a token of good faith?"

"That's what I said."

I let out something long and irregular that may or may not sound like a sigh of exasperation at his end of the wire. At the same time, I want this Roberts character to understand he's not dealing with a bumpkin.

"Okay, Mr. Roberts, here's the gig. Give me Ms. Lasner's email address, I'll forward the picture to her tomorrow morning at ten o'clock sharp. At some time this afternoon, I'll send you the routing and account numbers of a little checking account I keep in the Canary Islands to meet my mid-winter vacation needs. That will give you plenty of time to arrange for a transfer between ten o'clock and twelve o'clock sharp, tomorrow. That's twelve o'clock *noon,* Mr. Roberts.

"Once the money's in my account, I'll send you the studio shots, and our little transaction is finished. You never heard of me, I never heard of you."

"You trust me enough to send me the first picture before my money's in your account?"

"I do. However, the photo will be booby-trapped just to make sure you don't forget."

"Booby-trapped?"

"Computer viruses, Mr. Roberts? You've heard of 'em, no doubt. I'm telling you right up front that that photo will not be clean. However, it'll be clean enough to handle for exactly two hours. After that, if the hundred Gs aren't in my account, the photo and any copies you may *inadvertently* have made of it will disintegrate—as will your entire computer network."

"What if I choose not to open the file once you send it? What if I simply choose to drop the whole business right here and now?"

"You want to drop it?"

"I didn't say that. I was just exploring my options."

"As for not opening the file once I send it, you're a man of culture, Mr. Roberts. Maybe you've heard of Pandora's Box?"

"What if I don't like the photo?"

"You will, trust me." Silence. I prop my feet up on the desk to wait him out.

"Okay, listen to me. Send Laura your account information this afternoon and we'll look for your delivery by ten o'clock tomorrow morning. If we like what we see, you'll get your money by noon—and we'll expect to see delivery of the remaining photos by COB tomorrow. We got a deal?"

"We have a deal, Mr. Roberts. It's been a pleasure."

"Oh, no. The pleasure was *entirely* mine, I assure you. An account in the Canary Islands, huh? Don't tell me—you do comedy on the side."

And with that, he gives me Ms. Lasner's email address and I click off.

I'm now walking around my office "enumerating"—yeah, "enumerating" from Arthur was good—what remains for me to accomplish in the next few hours to earn my $100,000: get my two Yosemite shots of Angie developed, then get both of them—together with the contents of her book—transferred to a CD; buy myself a cheap laptop with the software and hook-up for a 'Net connection and with enough memory to store a dozen photographs; transfer the photos from the CD to the laptop; send Ms. Lasner my account information; treat myself to dinner at a place with tablecloths and silver; and then, get a good night's sleep.

The virus I'm going to tack onto the CD? Yeah, well, nobody ever accused me of a lack of imagination, even if I don't actually know how to create one. But got him thinking, didn't I.

Tomorrow, following our little bit of business, I'll stroll over to the East River and dispose of the laptop, the CD and the cell phone. However, I may just make one of those photographs of Angie in Yosemite the new wallpaper on my desktop. A memento, a reminder—of something and someone who could've been *very* special. It's too bad—.

This last thought is abruptly interrupted by the sound of someone buzzing at the front door. Who? What? Where?—at *this* hour? I sit back down, quiet as done lunch. Still, I can't ignore it. Whoever's pushing that buzzer came here on a mission, knows I'm open for business, knows I can hear the sound of it just as well as he or she can. I've gotta do something, now, and stop hiding. Lack of action at a moment like this suggests culpability, something to conceal, something I'm running away from, trying to avoid—and I know I've got no such thing.

I leap out of my chair, go straight to the door and open it. Looking up at me with bright blue eyes from what can't be more than a height of 5'5" in sheer stocking feet, 5'7" in the right pair of pumps, I see a winsome little hayseed of a thing—all teeth, smiles and hands clasping a single suitcase. She's got that "just-blew-in-from-Kansas" look, and I wonder whether she thinks she's in Oz and I'm the wizard. What a delight! I think.

"Can I help you?" I ask.

She pulls a scrap of paper from her pocket. The dress she's wearing actually has pockets. Do they really still make 'em that way? I think as I put my fingertips to my mouth. "Is this the Seymour Modeling Agency?" she asks, pretty as a cygnet in spring.

"It is indeed. How can I help?"

She lays her suitcase down on the floor, unsnaps it, pulls out a photo album—the kind of thing a young girl might keep with pictures of her family, her friends, her pets—and hands it to me. "My girlfriend took most of 'em," she says as I flip through.

"Uh-huh," I say.

"I know my book needs a bit of work."

"Your book. Yes. A bit of work. Well," I say as I close it and look down into those bright blues—so full of promise, of innocence, dare I say of "contrition," though I doubt she's got anything just *yet* to feel contrite about—"perhaps we can do something about that. Please come in."

"Do you think Mr. Seymour would be willing to look at my book?" she asks as she lugs her suitcase into my office.

I stop dead in my tracks, turn 'round, give her my full attention. "I do. And he did."

She looks puzzled, then suddenly blushes. The blues go big as a Kansas sky.

"And may I ask the identity of the young lady whose portfolio I've just has the pleasure of viewing?"

131

Her blush turns to sunset. She clearly likes my use of the word "portfolio." "Daisy," she says. "Daisy Miller." Funny, I think. I haven't thought of Henry James since my Princeton days. "But the name I've chosen for my modeling career is 'Hope.' Do you think it fits? Do you think I look hopeful?"

"I do," I answer. "And I think what you could use right now, young lady — to give that career of yours a little boost — is some breakfast. I know a diner right down the street. What'd you say —" and I leave the invitation unfinished, as I sense from her smile the admiration, the gratitude, the complete faith and trust she's now willing to place in me. This, I think, could just be the start of something *quite* special.

Russell Bittner lives and writes on a tiny clod of an island off the East Coast of the United States. The island is called "Long" and his borough is called "Brooklyn." Like Hobbes, he believes that "life is short, brutish and nasty." He also believes, however, that art is long; and, with Donne, that no man is one, entire of itself – either an island or a work of art.

His prose, poetry and photography have been widely published both in print and on the Net.